"You are so beautif[...]
surprised for saying it [...]

"You have no right to say such a thing," she said in a strangled small voice.

He knelt beside her. "Don't I?"

She scrambled to a more respectable sitting position and hurried to cover her ankles, which had been revealed to his view. "Evan," she sighed, suddenly weary of him. "What do you want from me?"

"I do not know," he said. She knew that he spoke the truth. His eyes took on a troubled look as he reached out and caressed her cheek with the palm of his hand. The gentleness of his touch took her breath away and left her feeling weak and wanting.

"Perhaps this."

He leaned toward her. His lips touched hers only briefly and then he pulled back as if reconsidering his actions.

But she forged ahead. . . .

Don't miss Jenna Mindel's delightful Regencies

Labor of Love
"A delicious blend of gentle humor and poignant heartache."
—*Romantic Times*

Blessing in Disguise
"A delightful debut . . . [a] true reading pleasure."
—Jo Beverley

Miranda's Mistake

Jenna Mindel

A SIGNET BOOK

SIGNET
Published by New American Library, a division of
Penguin Putnam Inc., 375 Hudson Street,
New York, New York 10014, U.S.A.
Penguin Books Ltd, 80 Strand,
London WC2R 0RL, England
Penguin Books Australia Ltd, 250 Camberwell Road,
Camberwell, Victoria 3124, Australia
Penguin Books Canada Ltd, 10 Alcorn Avenue,
Toronto, Ontario, Canada M4V 3B2
Penguin Books (N.Z.) Ltd, Cnr Rosedale and Airborne Roads,
Albany, Auckland 1310, New Zealand

Penguin Books Ltd, Registered Offices:
Harmondsworth, Middlesex, England

First published by Signet, an imprint of New American Library,
a division of Penguin Putnam Inc.

First Printing, April 2003
10 9 8 7 6 5 4 3 2 1

To my parents, George and Judee Grodesky. Thank you for teaching me that there is no such thing as a dream *too big*. You have always been a source of encouragement and you have shown me how to live life filled with laughter and love. For that, I will always be grateful.

Chapter One

October 1818
Leicestershire

"*M*iranda, thank goodness you have come. I do not know what I would have done without you."

Miranda embraced her dear friend Beatrice, the Lady Rothwell, on the front steps of Rothwell Park. "I am quite happy to help."

Beatrice pulled back to look at her closely. "You do not mind, truly?"

She breathed in the crisp, clean air of the countryside and smiled. "Truly, I am glad to be here."

Beatrice hugged her again. "I was worried for you on your trip. I know you prefer London to the country. It has been a long time since you have visited."

Miranda squeezed her friend tighter, feeling a bit guilty. "Too long, I am afraid."

"Come." Beatrice ushered Miranda through the door. "Rothwell will actually join us for tea. Your luggage arrived yesterday, and no doubt Babette will wish to organize your things." Beatrice's servant quickly escorted Miranda's maid up the stairs.

Miranda followed Beatrice through the spacious

and well-appointed halls. She welcomed her friend's managing ways and suddenly felt quite at home. Miranda remembered when Beatrice, once her governess, had left Hemsley Manor to marry Lord Rothwell. It was just before Miranda had left for London and her first Season.

Lord Rothwell had chosen the very capable Beatrice as his wife with utmost faith that she could raise his daughter to become a proper young lady. Miranda had been asked to Rothwell Park to expand upon Beatrice's work.

Artemis Rothwell had followed too closely in her papa's footsteps, much to Beatrice's chagrin. The girl was too fond of outdoor activities, too intelligent, and too plain. Miranda had been sent for to see what could be done in little more than two weeks before several families descended upon Rothwell Park for a hunting party.

They entered a cozy drawing room with a fire crackling in the grate. Several paintings of hunting scenes graced the walls, in addition to a musket collection. Lord Rothwell lounged in an overstuffed chair by the fire. Miranda could keep from smiling as she noted that he had not changed out of his riding clothes. His boots held traces of mud, and his eyes were closed.

"Beldon!" Beatrice scolded.

He nearly jumped at his wife's voice.

"You could have changed, dear," Beatrice said.

"Miranda doesn't mind, do you?" he asked, after he stood and stretched.

"No, of course not." She laughed out loud when he scooped her up for a big embrace that left her breathless. Lord Rothwell was a large man with a heart nearly as enormous.

"How are you?" he asked her once he placed her back on her feet.

"I am well, Rothwell. Beatrice tells me you have invited half the *ton* here for the hunt."

"As usual, she exaggerates." He gave his wife a playful wink. "I have invited only a few eligible young men and some acquaintances along with their wives and daughters."

"You see?" Beatrice quipped.

Miranda laughed again and it felt good. She had not been to Rothwell Park since her father had died six years ago. That had been the last time she had been home, too. She had come to terms with her decision to marry the Earl of Crandle seven years ago, but returning to the country always swamped her with feelings of regret for the life she had left behind.

She shook off her melancholy thoughts and helped Beatrice, as she poured the tea. She was Miranda's only true friend. Beatrice visited her every year in London, and the two had exchanged letters for years. "How are Artemis and the boys?"

"The twins are on their Grand Tour, no doubt causing trouble all over the Continent," Rothwell said. "Little Harry and Julian are at Eton. They will come home at Christmastide and Artemis . . . well—" Rothwell turned to his wife. "How should we explain Artemis?"

"I saw her not two years ago," Miranda said. "She is a dear child. Surely she is well."

"Hale and hearty." Rothwell accepted his tea from Beatrice.

Beatrice handed a cup to Miranda. "What he is trying to say is that Artemis is showing her stubbornness right now. She is refusing a Season."

"Part of this is your fault," Rothwell said to his wife with good humor. "It's all those blasted books you have let her read—Mary Wolstencraft and such nonsense."

Miranda looked at Beatrice.

"It is not quite as simple as that. Artemis cried off from a Season last year. We did not wish to push her, but now she is swearing off marriage altogether. She has taken some of Wolstencraft's beliefs to the extreme. I have taught Artemis the delicate arts of watercolor and such, but in them she has no interest. She cares only to loiter about the stables. I do not quite know what to do with her. She turned nineteen this past summer, and it is time she gave some thought to a life of her own. I thought you might help. She has always admired you."

Miranda sipped her tea. "I see. Does she know why I have come?"

Beatrice and Rothwell looked decidedly guilty. "I thought we should surprise her," Beatrice said. "Besides, I could use your help as well. You are quite used to entertaining the multitudes."

"I shall do my best. Where is she?"

"Where is who?" Artemis Rothwell entered the room with a broad grin.

"Why, you, of course! Now, come." She held out her arms.

"Miranda!" Artemis bounded across the room. "When did you arrive? I thought you were coming later with the rest of the guests."

Miranda stood her ground but was nearly knocked over by the tall young lady that embraced her. "My goodness." She pulled back, her hands resting high upon Artemis' shoulders. "Let me look at you. You have grown considerably since the last time you were in London." Miranda realized she had said the wrong thing when the light dimmed in Artemis' eyes.

"I am rather a giantess, am I not?"

"Just like your papa," Rothwell beamed.

Miranda felt her heart twist. It was obvious the girl was uncomfortable with her size. "You do your name proud. You look like an Amazon huntress." Miranda patted Artemis' back. "There is no need to slouch. Now, come and help me find where Babette put everything. You must tell me all the local gossip." Miranda winked across the room at a smiling Beatrice. She would not fib about the reason she had come early. "And I shall show you any number of devices that will impress your guests."

A look of wariness stole over Artemis. "My mother wheedled you into this, didn't she? I do not wish to be remodeled into a simpering miss casting lures out to hapless males. I am the equal of any man who's been invited here. I'll not make a fool of myself trying to attract their attention." She folded her arms with a rebellious sniff.

Miranda realized that she had much work ahead of her. "Of course not, dear. But there is an art to being a woman. Consider me an artist working with an excellent palette of paints. We need only put them to use on canvas."

Artemis looked skeptical.

Miranda noticed that Beatrice had set down her tea. She patted her husband's arm to keep him quiet. "Come, Artemis, let us both show Miranda to her room."

Two weeks later Evan Langley, Earl of Ashbourne rode quietly along the lane. He was early for the house party, he knew, but then Rothwell had expressly asked him to come a couple days beforehand. He let out a sigh.

It was time he set up his nursery. If Rothwell's daughter proved willing, he'd marry the girl and be done with it. He had no desire to go to London for the Season. He had no taste for it—not anymore, not after Miranda.

He wondered why, after all this time, he had thought of her. He had effectively kept her out of his mind for a few years now. Perhaps it was his plans to wed that forced her memory to plague him. He experienced the familiar pang somewhere in the region of his heart that always stabbed him when he thought of her.

Evan had done his best to become the logical man he wanted to be. He alone controlled his destiny, his life, and his feelings. But it never failed to annoy him that the memory of Miranda Hemsley unsettled him. After all these years, she still had a hold on him.

"What has you so glum?"

Evan turned to his friend and fellow huntsman, George Clasby. "Nothing, really."

"Come now, it's not like you to be so quiet. This is the *Quorn* we are riding in little more than a week. I hear Rothwell has horses fit for the Prince Regent himself."

"He has the finest stables in England," Evan said, with deep appreciation.

"I've also heard his daughter could be kept there too. She's quite the horsewoman but not nearly so fair to look upon."

"I have met her only once. She might be considered a bit plain, but I cannot think she will mind staying in the country to raise a brood of heirs for the Ashbourne title." Evan shifted in his saddle. He and Clasby had chosen to ride the half-day journey to Rothwell Park. The carriage with their luggage and valets lagged behind.

"Ashbourne, there are any number of ladies who would drop dead this minute to be your countess. I don't understand why you simply don't come with me to London."

"I do not like London." Again Evan shifted in the saddle.

"So you have said before."

Evan ignored the look his friend cast him. "What of you? You travel to town every Season, and still you have not wed. Who is it that you search for?"

"If I knew that, it would not be nearly so entertaining to sample the possibilities."

Evan shook his head. "You are a reprobate through and through."

Evan had been hunting with George Clasby for years, ever since Evan inherited the Ashbourne title and manor. Clasby's lands bordered his own, and the two had become fast friends hunting grouse.

Evan had become an earl through a series of mishaps that ended in the deaths of each heir to the Ashbourne line before him. He had inherited a heavily mortgaged estate that had been sadly neglected. It did not take him long to dismiss the dishonest bailiff and sell his London town house to pay down his new debts.

After five years of concentrated effort, Evan had restored Ash Manor and its vast land holdings to their rightful glory—and to profitable farming. He was proud of his accomplishment, and he wasn't about to leave his self-made legacy to someone who could destroy what he had worked so hard to bring about.

He'd not leave his title to anyone other than the fruit of his own loins. He needed a son he could raise in his own image. At thirty-four, he was not getting younger. The time to marry was at hand.

"I want to fall madly in love," George said. "I have no need of wealth or status. I am completely content as I am, but I should like to fall in love. I have yet to experience true love."

"It is not all that it is hailed to be."

"Love?"

"Precisely." Evan nearly gritted his teeth. "Trust me, you will rue the day it happens."

"My word, Ashbourne! You are against falling in love!" Clasby looked genuinely aghast. "There can only be one reason. You have loved and lost. I had no idea."

"It is not something a man parades about. I was young and quite foolish. I did not realize the way of the world then. I do now."

"Pray, enlighten me," Clasby asked with a grin.

"Don't be a dolt. You know the ways of women and their greedy hearts. Have you not escaped from the clutches of a fortune hunter or two?"

"They cannot all be that way."

"Can they not?" Evan asked.

It had been two long weeks, and Miranda had made only small improvements in Artemis. She and Beatrice had coaxed their young charge into dancing only to suffer from bruised toes. Miranda had shown Artemis how to walk like a lady, but the child continued to move with long, aggressive strides. Lord Rothwell was no help. He only laughed at their efforts, much to his wife's annoyance.

"You have been a great help to Mama," Artemis said, as she looked out of the window of Miranda's room.

"It is nothing, really." Miranda tried to tuck wisps of her hair back into the tight knot Babette had begrudgingly formed this morning. Her maid was used to styling her mistress' hair in much more elaborate styles. She was sorely distressed when Miranda had asked for something simple.

"But it is." Artemis came away from the glass to sit upon the bed in the pool of sunshine streaming into the room. "We have never had so many grand folk stay with us before. Papa is not much of a society man, and Mama is nervous about making him proud."

Miranda turned away from the mirror, her hair momentarily forgotten. "But they have been invited to the finest homes in London. Your parents are much admired. There is nothing for them to prove."

"Mama thinks there is. Miranda, you opened many of those doors with your connections. Papa never went to London until after he married Mama."

Miranda sat down next to Artemis and stroked the girl's long dark hair that hung past her shoulders. She was of an age to put her hair up, but she continued to wear it loose. "You used to love to come to London to visit me. Why do you not wish to go in the spring and have a Season?"

"I will not be auctioned off to the highest bidder like a horse at Tattersall's," Artemis hissed.

"It is not like that. There are parties and balls and wonderful places to see."

"Pah." Artemis stood to pace the room. "I know

that my parents wish to see me wed. I am not stupid." She swung her arms open wide. "This whole house party is their attempt to bring the gentlemen to me, since I do not wish to go to them in London."

Miranda narrowed her gaze. She did not understand why a Season concerned Artemis so. "Does it not bother you to have them come here for your inspection?"

Artemis shook her head. "I am comfortable here. This is my home."

There was more to Artemis than met the eye. She was a warm and kindhearted young lady who doted on her family, as they doted on her. Rothwell had indulged his only daughter's every whim, but he also had treated her much as he did his sons. When he married Beatrice, Artemis was eleven years old and desperately in need of a feminine influence.

Although Beatrice made an excellent role model, she had instilled her own ideas of women's independence into her stepdaughter. The two of them had created a young woman who straddled the lines of what was masculine and feminine. Artemis was an enigma and she believed that if she left the safety of her own home, she might be ridiculed for her unusual ways.

Miranda was not about to let that happen. She had tried to teach Artemis to move with grace and dignity. There was no reason the girl could not make a good match. Miranda was determined to equip her with the tools needed to capture the attentions of the man of her choice. Artemis deserved a love match.

Artemis stopped pacing to look out the window that overlooked the vast drive and the valley beyond. "Oh my goodness, he's here!"

"Who's here?" Miranda joined her at the window.

"Lord Ashbourne. He is one of the best riders in the county. I knew Papa had invited him, but I never expected him this early. I cannot wait to ride with him and test his mettle."

Miranda saw two gentlemen approaching on horseback. Both appeared to be well appointed, but she could not distinguish their features because of the distance. "How do you know it is he?"

"Do you see the hunter he rides? Papa sold it to him this spring. Paid a pretty price, he did. I'd know that horse anywhere."

Miranda smiled, but there was something almost familiar about this Lord Ashbourne. She did not know the name, nor did she recall ever meeting this man in London. She stepped away from the curtains without giving the man another thought. "Come, Artemis, let us go to your room. We must choose which of your new gowns you shall wear for dinner."

Dinner would be served shortly. Miranda instructed the housekeeper to set two more place settings, while Beatrice checked with Cook on the additional food needed. Rothwell had not informed his wife of his early invitation to the gentlemen. Miranda waited in the drawing room with a nervous hostess.

"I do hope Artemis behaves herself." Beatrice paced the floor, wringing her hands nervously.

"She will. She is quite looking forward to meeting this Lord Ashbourne. She tells me he is an expert rider." Miranda smoothed the folds of her carefully chosen russet silk gown. She had brought with her mainly modest gowns of simple styling so as not to compete with either of the Rothwell ladies.

"You have been so good for Artemis," Beatrice

said. "I know Beldon and I have indulged her more than perhaps was good for her, but she is our only daughter, after all."

"You have done an excellent job of raising her. Artemis is a sensitive and caring child. Underneath her rough and tumble exterior is a heart of pure gold."

Voices in the hall announced the gentlemen, and Miranda prepared herself by affixing her society smile. Rothwell led the men into the room.

"Ashbourne, I thank you for your praise of my stables; perhaps you might ride one of my horses during the hunt," Rothwell said.

Miranda looked up, and her smile died upon her lips. Her eyes widened, and she felt the blood drain from her face. She leaned against the library table, grateful for something solid to hold her upright.

In walked Evan Langley, the man she had jilted seven years ago—the only man she had ever loved.

Quickly, she closed her mouth and tried to quell her rapidly beating heart. Panic seized her. What should she say to him? She had not spoken a word to him; she had not even seen him since she broke his heart with the news of her marriage to Lord Crandle. What on earth was he doing here?

Evan bent to kiss Beatrice's hand in greeting. He had not noticed her yet.

"And this is my wife's dearest friend, Lady Crandle," Rothwell introduced them. "Miranda, this is Lord Ashbourne, and this is Mr. Clasby."

Miranda watched the warmth in Evan's gray eyes disappear as recognition dawned in his gaze. With an icy coldness he looked directly into her eyes. "Lady Crandle, how nice to meet you."

"Lord Ashbourne," she breathed. When had he become a *Lord?* "Mr. Clasby," she added with a nod.

Mr. Clasby, she noted, glanced between Evan and her until Rothwell pulled him away to show him a huge stag's head mounted upon the wall. Evan stayed where he was, much to Miranda's dismay. She feared she had not recovered from the shock of seeing him. Her mouth had gone completely dry, and she hadn't an intelligent thought in her head.

"Miranda," he said quietly, "it has been a long time."

"Indeed it has." He wore his hair much shorter than before. The soft dark curls she used to love to twine about her fingers had been shorn off.

"You look well," he said.

"As do you, Lord Ashbourne." His handsome looks had only improved with age. "And may I congratulate you upon securing a title?" Somehow her words sounded terribly inappropriate.

He narrowed his gaze. "Unfortunate that I received it so late."

"Yes." She did not miss the insult he cast at her.

"So, how is old Crandle?" he asked, pleasantly enough, as if their sudden meeting after seven years meant nothing to him.

"Crandle is dead," she blurted. "He passed away a little over a year ago."

Surprise lit his features, only to be controlled into an iron-edged frown. "I did not know," he said. "Forgive me."

Miranda nodded, at a loss for what to say next.

Fortunately, Artemis chose that moment to enter the drawing room, relieving Miranda of having to respond. Miranda smiled with pride. Artemis, dressed in a simple gown of pale green muslin, looked very grown up indeed, with her hair piled high atop her head. Beatrice beamed as she introduced her daughter to Evan—Lord Ashbourne—and Mr. Clasby.

Artemis did not act the least bit shy or awkward. In fact, she held out her hand, as would any gentleman when meeting another gentleman. Miranda sighed. Although some of the rough edges had been smoothed, Artemis was still too forthright in her manners. Neither of the men appeared to mind. Each took their turn bowing over her extended hand, making the slight faux pas disappear entirely.

Miranda watched the introductions from afar, grateful for the reprieve. Evan looked older, of course, but he also appeared to have changed. Not surprising, she supposed, after seven years. The ready smile that used to hover at the corners of his mouth, accenting his dimples, was gone. A polite pursing of his lips had taken its place. His eyes, which had always been clear windows into his heart and soul, were now clouded and shuttered.

He carried himself with authority, as if he had been born and raised into a title, instead of inheriting one from a distant relative. And, yet, with all her connections in London, she had never heard about his new status. She had no idea when he had become Lord Ashbourne or how.

Rothwell came to stand beside her. "You have done well with Artemis, and I thank you."

Miranda wanted to explain that they were not yet finished but refrained when she saw the pride shining in Rothwell's eyes. The one thing she could never find fault with in either of Artemis' parents was their love for their daughter.

"Thank you."

"She will make the right man an admirable wife."
Rothwell's chest actually swelled as he spoke.

Miranda politely agreed, but Artemis did not appear overly interested in becoming a wife.

Dinner was announced, and Miranda breathed deeply. She was glad to quit the small drawing room. Evan's presence filled it too easily, causing Miranda to continually glance his way.

Rothwell and Beatrice led their guests to the dining room, Mr. Clasby offered her his arm, which she gladly took, but not before she saw the artificially sweet smile Evan bestowed upon Artemis before offering his arm to her.

It was then that it hit her. Evan had been invited for Artemis' sake. Rothwell's words echoed in her ears. *"She will make the right man an admirable wife."*

Miranda's appetite was lost as she considered that Evan had been approved as just such a man.

Chapter Two

*E*van watched Miranda. He could not help it. She was still beautiful, perhaps more so than he remembered. Her thick auburn hair still shone with glimmers of gold. Age appeared not to have touched her face or her delectable form. The only difference he could detect in her was a guarded distance in her eyes. And Crandle was dead.

Never had he expected to see her again—and especially not at Rothwell Park. Although highly respected and wealthy in his own right, Lord Rothwell rarely spent time in London. He preferred life in the country, as did Evan. Miranda, however, moved in the highest circles of society. Crandle had seen to that. After Miranda left Evan, he swore an oath never to return to London and be part of a world full of title-hunting girls and their matchmaking mamas. He did not care to admit that his real reason was to avoid seeing Miranda as Lady Crandle. Even so, their paths had finally crossed, and Evan found himself ill-prepared for it.

He glanced at Miss Artemis Rothwell, who sat next to him. She chattered on about the upcoming hunt with such excitement that he felt a smile tug at his mouth. She was not a beauty, and that pleased him.

She was not the kind of female to incite the burning insanity he had experienced with Miranda.

"How do you like that hunter Father sold to you?" Miss Rothwell asked.

"Elias is superb," Evan answered, before sipping his wine.

"Will you use him in the Quorn?"

"I plan to, for the first few days, at least. I brought additional horses with me to use as well, unless your Father prefers that I ride one of his."

"I should love to go," Miss Rothwell whispered.

Her mother heard her. "Ladies cannot ride in the Quorn." Lady Rothwell looked to Miranda for help.

"It would be dangerous," Miranda said.

"But I can handle myself on a horse better than many men I've seen," Miss Rothwell argued.

"Of course you can," Miranda agreed softly, "but ladies might prove to be a distraction to the men."

"Exactly so," Mr. Clasby added. "I'd break my neck clearing a hedge if I had my eyes on a lady as appealing as you, Miss Rothwell."

"Well, I have never heard of anything so silly." Miss Rothwell colored pink about the cheeks before turning her attention to her roasted grouse.

Evan studied Miranda, who sat directly across the table from him. He was surprised when she did not immediately look away. He wondered how she had become close to this warm family who rusticated in the Midlands year round. She did not quite fit into the relaxed atmosphere. He felt the tension in her.

"Lady Crandle," he started, "do you come to Rothwell Park often?"

He saw that his question made her uncomfortable. She took her time wiping her mouth with her napkin before answering. "Not often, no."

"I see," he said.

She did not appear eager for conversation, and so he turned back to Miss Rothwell, the young lady he planned to court. Besides, Clasby took up where he had failed and drew Miranda out, discussing the latest gossip regarding the Little Season.

Dinner proceeded until the ladies left the men to their port. They did not linger overlong, so the men joined the women in the drawing room after only one glass.

Evan chose a chair next to the fire beside Miranda, while the others played a game of whist. His curiosity about her fairly begged to be satisfied. What had she been doing these last seven years? "Do you not play cards, Lady Crandle?" he asked.

"I have never been fond of cards," she responded with complete reserve, although her eyes narrowed slightly.

He affected her, he could tell. He took some bitter sense of pleasure in that. For some reason, he wanted to make her uncomfortable. Part of him wanted to punish her for what she had done to him. "What brings you here? I did not realize that you knew the Rothwells."

"Beatrice, Lady Rothwell, was once my governess," she said. "We have remained close over the years. She asked that I help Artemis with some of the usual feminine accomplishments. So I came here to offer my aid." She looked down at her hands held firmly clasped in her lap.

Evan stared at her long, slim fingers with their delicately shaped nails. He had often held those hands when they had been together. It had been near impossible not to touch one another then. He quickly looked away.

"I see," he finally said. "Introduce her to several eligible men in a setting where she will no doubt show to advantage. Very clever indeed."

A delicate frown marred her perfect face, but she said nothing, and Evan felt annoyed. What would move this woman to speak to him? "Perhaps you might find an eligible gentleman as well," he said.

That garnered a reaction. Her beautiful hazel eyes darkened with indignation, though she remained outwardly calm. "That is not my intention, Lord Ashbourne."

"I beg your pardon." He fingered his chin. "I meant no offense." But he had. In fact, he wanted to say something that would crack her cold reserve. "No doubt it is much too soon after your beloved husband's death to be thinking of such things."

His sarcasm was not lost on her. He received yet another flash of fury, but that was all. No set downs, which he deserved. Such self-control was admirable.

She turned to look into the fire, cutting off any further discussion between them. Perhaps she did not care a whit about him, and that was why she showed no reflection of the tumultuous emotions bubbling through him at this moment.

Egad! Despite his efforts to forget about her all these years, he still felt an attraction toward her. It pumped through his veins, even now, burning his insides. She had always done that to him.

He had sworn he'd never allow a woman to get under his skin as Miranda Hemsley had done. And there she sat calmly next to him, as if he were nothing more than an annoyance to her. She deserved to be punished for what she had done to him, did she not? Perhaps he could toy with her just enough to knock aside the haughtiness she displayed. It would no doubt do her some good. The pinched expression she wore did not look well on her. In the process, he might just rid himself of the effect she had on him. He had made himself into a man who completely controlled his every action. Why not test that control and prove that he had conquered the weaknesses of his past once and for all?

Miranda wished Evan would just go away and leave her alone. Her insides quaked with the desire to study him, but she could not do so under his nose. She had not forgotten how handsome he was, but seeing him in the flesh was another matter entirely. She had kept the memory of his carefree and flirtatious manner as if it were sacred. The arrogant lord next to her was completely at odds with the Evan she had once known.

Find an eligible gentleman, indeed! As if she ever would. There was no one eligible for her, not anymore. She felt dried up inside like a winter apple left to rot. And rot is just what had happened to her these last seven years. All the love she had to give had been left to rot and die.

She wondered what he was thinking. She had not missed the jab he had directed at her about Crandle. She supposed she could not blame him. She had hurt him deeply when she suddenly married Crandle with little more than a curt excuse about her duty to her family. Perhaps now it was only his pride that smarted, but even so, she was sorry for it. She had paid the price in full with seven years of unhappiness.

She could not continue to ignore the man when he sat right next to her. Besides, she did not wish to rouse Beatrice's attention by being rude. No one need know what they had been to each other.

She steadied her nerves and turned to face him. "Lord Ashbourne, I have not seen you in London. What has kept you away? Business?" She had to own that she wished to know how it came about that he now had a title.

"Not business," he answered. "You."

She felt her mouth drop open. Surely he jested. "It is a big city, my lord."

"Not big enough," he answered quietly.

She swallowed the acid words resting upon her tongue. Taking three calming breaths, Miranda acted as if nothing was amiss in their conversation. "Aside from avoiding my presence," she said with almost gentle humor, "what else have you been about?"

She saw admiration in his eyes and let herself relax somewhat. "I have been exceptionally busy with my estates," he said. He looked hesitant to continue, as if weighing his options. But then he too relaxed. He leaned back in his chair and stretched his muscular legs out in front of him, crossing his ankles.

"Inheriting Ash Manor and all the properties that came with the title has kept my days fully occupied, I assure you."

She tried to ignore the delightful shape of his calves that showed to advantage in the white stockings he wore. He needed no padding there; she clearly saw the indentations of taut muscle. Distracted, she said, "I do not recall hearing news of you coming into an inheritance."

"It had been transferred so many times to so many uncles and cousins that by the time I became heir, no one cared." He smiled, and her insides melted.

Evan Langley had a smile that softened the hardest of hearts, regardless of gender. He had dimples on both sides of his mouth that irreverently deepened whenever he laughed or smiled. Those dimples had gotten him out of several coils and even a duel or two. She remembered the countless stories he had told her.

She bit her bottom lip to keep from smiling like a moonstruck ninnyhammer. "I see."

Again they settled into an uncomfortable silence. The sounds of the others playing a rousing game of whist served only to accentuate the quiet that had fallen between them. The fire crackled and sizzled, calling their attention to the warm flow of heat that emanated from the grate.

Evan cleared his throat. "How are your parents?"

Miranda suspected that he did not give two sheets what the answer was, but even so she struggled with her answer. Talking of such things brought back too many memories she had tried to bury. "Papa died nearly six years ago. My mother is well. She lives in the dower house at Hemsley. My brother and his family reside in the main house."

"I see." He tapped his fingers along the arm of his chair. "I am sorry to hear about your father. He was a kind man."

Another stretch of silence.

Miranda could take it no more. She stood.

Evan was on his feet in a trice.

"I shall bid you good evening, Ashbourne," she said, with a heavy accent upon his title. "It has been rather a long day."

"Of course." He bowed.

She thought she might have mistaken the look of disappointment in Evan's eyes. Whatever it was that she thought she saw, it was gone in moments.

She made her rounds of the whist table and left the drawing room, grateful to be gone from Evan's unnerving presence. As she left, she wondered what it might have been like had they married as once intended. Would they have sat together at night in comfortable silence and watched the fire's glow? Would they have had children? She suffered a deep ache in the region of her heart. She breathed an irritated sigh. She must not think such impossible thoughts, since they brought only pain and regret for what might have been.

Evan tossed and turned until finally he could take it no more. He threw back the coverlet and swung his bare legs over the side of the bed. His timepiece read three o'clock, yet he had not slept a wink. He needed something to drink. Slipping into his dressing gown, he padded barefoot across the floor. Rothwell was bound to have something.

Careful to tread quietly, Evan made his way down the stairs into his host's study, where he poured himself a healthy portion of brandy. There was no point in returning to his room, since he doubted sleep would come any time soon. He ventured down the hall, glass in hand, to the cozy drawing room. The glowing red embers of the banked fire beckoned to him. He pulled a chair close to the hearth and settled into it to enjoy his spirits. He hoped the mixture of brandy and warmth would make him sleepy.

A sudden gasp and the crash of shattered glass upon the floor had him to his feet with a start. "What—who's there?" he hissed.

"It is Miranda," she whispered. "You frightened the wits out of me. What are you doing here?" She stood in the doorway, looking as if she too had sought the solace of the drawing room.

"I could ask the same of you," he said with barely

concealed frustration. He was in no mood to endure the company of the very reason for his lost sleep. She had been in his thoughts since she had left this very room earlier that night. The fact that she stood in her night rail with her hair loosed and falling freely about her shoulders did nothing to improve his disposition.

"I could not sleep, if you must know," she said as she stooped down to pick up shards of broken glass.

"Devil a bit! Don't go poking about in that glass; you will cut yourself. Let me call for a servant."

She ignored him and continued to pick up the glittering pieces.

He hurried to light an oil lamp with one of the fireplace tinder sticks and brought it to where she crouched upon the floor. "Miranda, your feet are bare. Back away and let me call for a servant."

"They will have enough to do when the other guests arrive; let them sleep."

He was surprised at her concern for the staff. He would have thought that, after years in Crandle's lofty presence, care for the sleep of servants would have been lost to her. "Here, step aside, and let me clean this up, then."

"You have bare feet, too," she told him.

With a sigh, he squatted down across from her to help. "Here." He handed her a silver tray. "Put the glass on this."

"Very well." She dumped a handful of it onto the tray with a rattle.

"You could not sleep?" Evan asked.

"No."

"Why not?"

She looked completely offended at his forward-ness. "I do not think it any of your concern." Another rattle.

"Were you, perhaps, thinking of me?" He wanted to fluster her, make a dent in her shield of haughty reserve.

Her eyes flashed. "You have become quite filled with your own consequence since obtaining a title, I think."

He laughed aloud. "And what of you? You, too, have changed."

"Perhaps I have, just as all people do with time. Why should that surprise you?"

He looked away from her to concentrate on picking up the pieces of glass. "I imagine that living with Crandle would make anyone change." He still had trouble accepting the fact that she had jilted him to marry a man three times her age, simply for his wealth and title.

She quickly dropped more glass onto the tray. "Crandle exposed me to many things. I do not think it odd that I developed into something other than what I once was."

He stilled her hands. "There was nothing wrong with the way you were," he whispered. Storm clouds rolled about in her eyes, but her composure did not falter.

"And what of you?" she asked. "You are not the same man I once knew."

"No, thankfully, I am not." His voice was laced with sarcasm.

"What does that mean?" She roughly grabbed a piece of glass. "Ouch." She sat back on her knees and held her pierced finger as it turned red with blood.

"Here, let me see." He tried to take her hand, but she pulled it out of his grasp.

"I am fine."

"Give me your hand," he said with firmness. He'd not have her bleed all over her frilly white gown.

She thrust out her hand for his inspection.

He held the lamp close to inspect the tiny cut that glimmered in the light. "There's a piece stuck in there." He set down the lamp, and pulled a handkerchief from the pocket of his robe. "This might hurt a bit."

"Very well," she said, with a sigh. She would not look at him, though.

He took her finger, and with his handkerchief over his own fingers, he squeezed until the tiny piece of glass bled free of her skin. He wiped the rest of the blood away. "There, I have it."

Her eyes looked suspiciously bright. Surely he could not have hurt her.

"Thank you," she said softly.

She tried to pull her hand free, but he did not let go. He stroked her palm with his thumb. They both knelt upon the floor, so close to one another that their knees practically touched. Her hair shone with shimmers of gold light from the fire, and he longed to run his hands through it and feel the texture. He panicked before he acted on his desire, and the moment was lost.

"There," he said, as he quickly wrapped the cloth around her finger. "Keep that tight, and it should stop bleeding."

"I thank you."

He picked up the silver tray filled with glass and stood. "I shall take care of this. You may return to your bed."

She did not move. She sat back on her heels and

looked up at him. Evan looked down at the incredibly beautiful woman kneeling at his feet and wondered why he did not do something to take advantage of the situation. But this was Miranda. It scared the wits out of him that she still affected him. His body seemed totally disconnected from his mind and the painful memories it housed of the heartache this woman had caused him.

She stood suddenly, as if catching herself staring at him. She brushed out the front of the voluminous white gown she wore under a matching robe of the same fabric. "I bid you good night, Lord Ashbourne." She turned and left.

"Sleep well," he whispered once she had gone. He returned to his chair in front of the dying fire.

Miranda hurried out of the small drawing room, her heart beating wildly. She looked down at her finger, still wrapped in the white linen handkerchief with his initials embroidered on the corner. She stared at the letters *E* and *L*—Evan Langley—until she gave herself a mental shake.

She dared not bump into him again in the hallway. She would appear a complete fool standing there gazing at her finger. She dashed up the stairs as quietly as she could. Once in her room, she shut the door and leaned against it.

She was not in the least prepared for what had transpired between them. When he had held her hand, she thought she would melt into a puddle upon the floor, like the milk she had spilled.

She knew how to deal with forward men. She had become adept at sidestepping any and all advances made toward her. Crandle had taught her well how to handle the lower classes and what he called mush-rooming upstarts that would seek her favor simply because of her status.

He had also kept a strict watch upon her daily activities—whom she saw and why. Even had she wanted to have an illicit encounter, she would have been found out. It did not ever matter; entertaining cicisbei had never been something she was comfort-able with. She had remained a respectable wife of utmost dignity.

She unraveled the linen to check the cut on her finger. It bled no more. The crimson stain left behind on Evan's handkerchief reminded her too well of how she had broken the man's heart. He was no doubt over that, but his wounded pride remained, which explained his arrogance toward her.

What she could not explain was how quickly Evan had made her pulse race again, just by touching her. Seven years had not dulled the effect he had upon her body. Seven years in a chaste marriage made feelings she had thought long since buried burst frighteningly back into life.

Chapter Three

*E*van put down his comb and looked in the mirror while his valet brushed off his shoulders and pulled at his tight fitting coat. He thought he looked his very best. He stood staring at his reflection, wondering why he even cared. It was for Miranda that he had dressed with such care, and that made him angry.

There had to be a way to purge her from his thoughts once and for all. He had spent considerable time reinventing himself after she had jilted him. It was at that lowest point in his life that he decided he would no longer allow himself to be ruled by his emotions.

He had always been a hotheaded youth, a man given to fits of temper or passion. Miranda had inspired both in him, along with a possessiveness that bordered on obsession. And now, he had subconsciously dressed to please her. It was not to be borne. He needed to take control of the situation and turn the tables somehow. He needed to prove to himself that he was in control, that he would not revert to the man he once was.

The question was how.

He left his bedchamber, still contemplating his situation as he made his way to the morning room for breakfast. Lord and Lady Rothwell were already seated, as were Clasby, Miss Rothwell, and Miranda.

"Forgive my tardiness," Evan said, as he sat down across from Miss Rothwell.

"No need," Rothwell said. "We have only just started. Do help yourself to the sideboard, Ashbourne. Everything is fresh and hot."

"Thank you." He rose to do as bidden and saw Miranda had no food. On impulse he bent close to her. "May I fill your plate, Lady Crandle?" He took her plate in his hands.

She looked surprised but again masked any discomfort with the haughty reserve that grated on him. "Some eggs, I think, and perhaps a muffin," she said, as if speaking to a footman. "Thank you."

He bowed. "Miss Rothwell," he asked. "May I offer you anything?"

"More muffins, if you please," she said, her mouth nearly full.

He stifled a smile when he saw the scolding glare Miranda sent her. "Of course."

He filled each request, then returned to fetch his own plate. Inhaling the luscious smells of sausage and ham, he could feel his mouth water. He would no doubt eat very well at Rothwell Park.

"I say," Clasby started. "I hear there are the ruins of a medieval castle not far from here."

"Not far at all," Lady Rothwell concurred. "Ashby Castle is a mere seven miles west."

"Mama," Miss Rothwell said, "perhaps we might take a ride there to tour the grounds and climb the Hastings Tower."

"Aye," Lord Rothwell agreed. "I'll send a message

there straightaway and see if we can't ride over this afternoon."

Clasby smiled. "Excellent. I have a great love for history."

"Do you?" Lady Rothwell looked very pleased, and the two launched into a discussion while Miss Rothwell and her papa made plans for the outing.

"Will you go?" Evan asked Miranda.

"Of course." Her tone was matter of fact, until she quickly added, "Do not say that my attendance will keep you from going."

"Of course not." He wanted her to go; indeed he needed to be in her company in order to prove to himself that he could overcome his attraction to her.

Breakfast ended, and everyone scattered in different directions. Rothwell took Clasby under his wing to visit the terrierman who had been hired to flush out the fox before the hunt at Quorn next week. Evan declined to go. He was tired and he thought he would take a nap. Lady Rothwell had household business to attend to, and he was not sure where Miranda and Miss Rothwell had gone.

He finished his coffee in solitude, then left in search of a book from the Rothwell library.

"Must we do this again?" Artemis complained.

"Yes, we must. There is the Quorn ball, and before that, there will be dancing here. You will want to dance, I promise you." Miranda blew a stray piece of hair out of her face as she looked up at Artemis. "Now, let us start again, and, this time, let me lead."

"I shall try," Artemis mumbled, as she looked down to watch her feet.

A servant played the required notes for a waltz,

practically plucking out one key at a time, but the beat was right. Miranda whirled a stiff Artemis around the room, only to suffer sore toes.

"I just can't do it," Artemis said through gritted teeth.

"Yes, you can. You simply need to feel the music and glide with it." Just then the servant hit a sour note at the pianoforte, and Miranda winced.

"Problems?" Evan appeared in the doorway, an amused look upon his face.

She wanted to wipe away those devastating dimples, but instead, she appealed to him for help. "Ev— Lord Ashbourne! Yes, if you please, do help us. If you could partner Artemis, I shall play the pianoforte. Artemis is learning the steps to the waltz."

"Gladly." He walked over to Artemis and bowed before holding out his arms.

Artemis flushed several shades of pink, but at least she did not balk or run from the room.

"Are we ready then? A waltz," Miranda announced as she took the servant's place and began to play.

"I am not much for dancing," Artemis explained.

"You needn't worry. Do just as Lady Crandle instructed. Relax and listen to the music. I shall lead."

Miranda watched the pair move tentatively at first. Evan, an excellent dancer, led Artemis gently but firmly about the room. Although Artemis was a couple of inches taller, Evan was much more of a height to lead her than Miranda. It made a considerable difference. Artemis soon followed his steps perfectly, and the two glided comfortably as a pair.

"Very good," Miranda cheered from across the room, as her fingers skimmed the keys. "See, my dear, you are incredibly agile. You dance beautifully when paired with the right partner."

Artemis beamed, and Miranda felt a swell of pride.

"Let us try a quadrille," Evan suggested, once the waltz was done.

Miranda played song after song, and Evan danced with Artemis, showing her the steps and praising her when she picked them up quickly. He laughed with her when she faltered, rather than at her. He did his best to make Artemis feel at ease, and Miranda was delighted at his generosity. The look of confidence on Artemis' face when they finished was priceless.

Artemis smiled shyly when she thanked Evan before scurrying off to change into her riding habit for the picnic that was to be enjoyed on the way to Ashby Castle. They were to leave in an hour.

Miranda became very still when Evan walked toward her. They were completely alone in the large ballroom. "Thank you," she said.

"She's a charming girl," he said with wonder.

"Of course she is. You seem surprised."

"I just—" he looked almost sheepish. "She has a severe look to her."

Miranda nodded. "She will soften."

"Is she your clay, then? Will you remake her into your own image?" he asked.

He was serious, and she felt suddenly defensive. "I am simply trying to ease her way. Beatrice wanted me to help with some of the finer points."

"No doubt you learned much about the *fine* points of living with Crandle."

Miranda shut the cover of the pianoforte with a snap. "What is it that you are trying to say? It is true. I learned much about society and the arts while living with Crandle. Is it so bad to better oneself?"

"What is wrong with Miss Rothwell as she is?" He stepped closer to her.

"Nothing!" His nearness nearly bowled her over. She could smell the light cologne he wore, and its scent beckoned to her. She took a step backward. "We just taught Artemis to dance with confidence. You see how tall she is. Her height makes her feel awkward performing the simple acts most ladies take completely in stride. What wrong do I do her by helping her feel more feminine?"

He narrowed his gaze. "There is nothing *un*feminine about Miss Rothwell," he countered.

"Perhaps to a man's point of view." Miranda slid past him to put away the sheet music in the cabinet against the far wall.

"Isn't that all that matters?"

She whirled around. "No, that is not all that matters. Ladies can be very cruel. I do not wish Artemis to feel the sting of a jealous young miss's remark about her lack of accomplishment. I shall see to it that Artemis prevails in that area."

"But her parents—"

She cut him off. "—have done an excellent job. Beatrice has honed that girl's mind into a sharp blade. Rothwell has given his daughter the advantage of outdoor pursuits and athleticism. I shall give her polish. I want her Season to be a success."

Evan looked thoughtful. "Rothwell said she doesn't want a Season."

"But she must have one," Miranda countered. She turned to find that Evan had followed her. He stood too close for her comfort.

"Why?" His gaze bored into her. "So that she can hunt for the highest and wealthiest title?"

"No." Miranda felt completely flustered.

"She's not your daughter, you know."

Miranda jerked back as if she'd been slapped. She loved Artemis like a daughter—the daughter she had never had the chance to have. "Of course I know that," her voice sounded hollow even to her own ears. "Why should you care what I am about?"

He shrugged his shoulders. "I don't."

Miranda brushed back another stray lock of hair. "Very well, then." There was nothing she could say after such an admission. "I must go and change. Thank you again for dancing with Miss Rothwell. I deeply appreciate your efforts," she said stiffly.

"The pleasure was entirely mine." He bowed as she walked past him.

His tone suggested something she feared she did not like. It did not matter. She needed to put some distance between them quickly before she said something she would no doubt regret. She was not trying to remake Artemis in her own image! Was she?

She shook her head. She must change into her riding clothes. She was not about to let Evan's words cause her a moment's doubt. She was doing what Beatrice and Rothwell wanted for their daughter. She was doing the best thing for the girl.

The afternoon proved perfect for the outing to the nearby castle ruins. The air was crisp but dry, with a warm sun shining from a cloudless sky. The autumn leaves had almost all fallen to the ground, making a carpet of burnished gold and rust. Evan breathed deeply of the fresh air. This was the life, he thought. He swore he was at his happiest when on horseback, trotting along in the beautiful countryside of the Midlands. Miss Rothwell made a dashing figure in a military-styled riding habit of dark brown. An aggressive rider, she dared him to race against her. Considering the leisurely pace the rest of the party kept, Evan thought it better to race on the way home. Miss Rothwell promised him that she would not forget.

Miranda, of course, looked ravishing in a dark green habit of the finest wool. He expected nothing less of her. She perched upon her sidesaddle with her back so stiff and straight that he feared she would be sore on the morrow. She rode tentatively, as if she was not entirely confident in her ability to stay mounted. He pulled up alongside her.

"Not used to riding?" he asked.

Her expression was unreadable, but she arched a perfectly shaped eyebrow at him. "I have not ridden in some time."

"Crandle?" He could not keep the word from escaping his lips. He did not quite understand why he felt the urge to taunt her so. He had practically accused her of overstepping her bounds where Miss Rothwell was concerned, and now he teased her about her lack of equestrian ability.

She had chosen the Earl of Crandle over him. Shameful though it was, he could not keep from rubbing it in every chance he got. Seeing her again had opened up the wound to his pride.

"Crandle kept an excellent stable," Miranda said, "but I rode only on occasion in Hyde Park when I was alone and could take my time."

Evan did not like the bitterness he detected in her eyes as she spoke. "I take it that Crandle did not often ride with you," he said quietly.

She reined in her horse and turned to face him. "Lord Ashbourne," she asked in a supercilious voice, "why the fascination with my late husband?"

The word *husband* echoed in his ears. *He* was supposed to have been her husband! "I beg your pardon, but is it not natural to wonder about the man who took you from me?"

"Perhaps you should just give over and leave it alone." She kicked the side of the chestnut mare she rode. The mare trotted obediently forward until Miranda slowed the horse on reaching Lady Rothwell.

Because I can't, Evan thought to himself. *I must know why you chose him over me.*

Rothwell rode up alongside him. "Come," he said. "The servants have gone ahead and prepared our luncheon. Let us arrange to arrive before the ladies so we can sample some of the food."

Evan grinned and followed his host as he spurred on his mount and overtook the ladies.

Miranda watched the gentlemen canter past her. Artemis took off at a near gallop to catch up to them. Beatrice, thankfully, remained at her side.

"Do you wish to stretch the horses' legs a bit? I know what Rothwell is up to."

"What is that?" Miranda asked.

"He will snatch the plum pudding before we arrive. If we do not race along, there will be none left for us!"

Miranda laughed. As wealthy a man as Rothwell was, he never acted puffed up. He was a country gentleman through and through, with an air of pure merriment about him. He was a happy man. "Very well, then, let us move along."

They urged their mounts into a canter and headed in the same direction as the men. Miranda enjoyed the pace but knew she would pay for it on the morrow. She would not for the world let Beatrice down, however. She hung on tightly and let the horse carry her along, grateful that she even managed to stay in the saddle.

They came upon a clearing atop the only hill overlooking the castle. The view was quite breathtaking. Miranda gazed in awe at the lush grounds leading to the ruins and the village of Ashby de la Zouch in the distance. She had expected a broken-down pile. There were turrets and walls of mellow-colored stone that reached up to the sky with regal majesty. Miranda imagined weary travelers welcomed into a Great Hall filled with lively music and noblemen and -women. It seemed to her like a fairy-tale place, and she was completely charmed.

"Oh, this is lovely!" she exclaimed.

"It is," Beatrice said. "A perfect day for a picnic and a tour, is it not? Especially before the hordes of guests arrive—we will have less opportunity for escapades, then."

Miranda nodded, but she was looking forward to the guests' arrivals. More visitors at Rothwell Park would make it easier to avoid Evan. They trotted up to the canopy set up by the servants, who had preceded them. True to Beatrice's words, Rothwell held a plate of plum pudding in his hands.

"Rothwell," Beatrice scolded softly as she slipped easily from her mount. "You had best save some of that for us." She tied her horse to the servants' carriage and hurried over to her husband.

Miranda hesitated in the saddle. She needed help to dismount, but she did not wish to call attention to her weakness amidst such experienced riders. As if sensing her distress, Evan walked toward her.

"May I be of assistance?"

"You need not bother; a servant can help me," she said, as frostily as she could. Her muscles already ached. It was difficult to be dignified when one's rump ached in protest at any further movement.

"The servants are busy preparing our meal." Evan reached up to her. A bold smile curved his lips, making his dimples dent deeply into his cheeks. He was indeed more handsome than he had any right to be. "Take my hand."

She took his hand and slid out of the saddle. She stumbled when her feet hit the ground, but Evan's arms were about her in a trice to steady her.

"Please," she whispered, suddenly breathless.

He looked into her eyes without letting go of her, and his eyes gleamed with a combination of mischief and desire.

She could not breathe. Time stood still, and all Miranda could hear was the erratic beating of her heart. It made no sense that after all these years he should enflame her senses just as he had always done. Panic took her, as she wondered who might have seen them, but her horse shielded them from the view of the others. "You may release me now," she said.

He colored slightly, but instead of letting go, he pulled her closer. "Perhaps I should show you what you chose to miss all these years."

She felt her cheeks grow hot. "You will not toy with me, Evan Langley."

"It's Lord Ashbourne, now, Miranda. And I think that I am only beginning to toy with you."

He let go of her abruptly, leaving her to catch her balance and her stolen breath. She had a premonition that the regret she had lived with these past seven years would seem as nothing compared with what Evan might inflict upon her over the next seven days.

If he wished to wage a war with her, then she would oblige him. Perhaps she might even come away free of the guilt and remorse that had been eating away at her spirit ever since she had left him. And perhaps she just might come away from this visit grateful for choosing Crandle, for once in her life.

She said nothing as he sauntered away from her. Pain shot through her hand, and she realized that she had been unconsciously wrapping her horse's reins around her hand so tightly that she had cut off the flow of blood to her fingers. She carefully unwound the leather and led her horse to the servants' carriage. She looped the reins through an iron ring, then patted the pretty mare's neck in an attempt to calm her raging emotions. She felt sick with feelings of anger-laced desire. How dare he!

"Are you all right, dear?" Beatrice asked quietly from behind her.

Miranda jumped from being startled. "I beg your pardon. I did not hear you." She turned to face her friend, knowing her face was flushed. "Yes, I am fine."

"Has Lord Ashbourne said something to upset you?"

Miranda did not wish to pull Beatrice into this when she had her hands full with the upcoming house party. Besides, Evan was her problem to deal with alone. "No," she answered quickly.

Too quickly, she realized, when Beatrice narrowed her gaze.

"Truly, Bea." Miranda looped her arm through her friend's. " 'Tis nothing. I simply needed to shake out my muscles a bit before I joined you. I did not wish to make Lord Ashbourne wait while I stretched." Her lie came too easily. She did not like having to tell it, but at least Beatrice was satisfied.

"Come, Cook has prepared a feast for us."

Miranda walked arm in arm with her friend. She laughed when Beatrice recounted how much pudding her husband had consumed since they arrived. "I do hope he has left some for me. It has been an age since I had plum pudding," Miranda said.

"Not a favorite of Lord Crandle's?" Beatrice asked innocently.

Miranda could have shrieked with frustration. She would just as soon forget her life with Crandle. There were some good things but on the whole, her marriage had been sadly lacking in all respects.

She had been kept as a possession prized for her beauty, as one would keep a valuable work of art. Crandle permitted nothing that might mar her looks. Her foods had been prepared by their cook under instruction to keep her slender. No puddings, no cakes or sweetmeats. She was allowed no overly strenuous activity that might cause her injury.

Miranda had been encouraged instead to develop her appreciation for the arts and the *haute monde*. Her social skills and feminine accomplishments were honed until she was sure she could quite outwatercolor the best of them. Her main escape had been in books. Crandle never censored her reading material. In this, he had been remiss: Miranda knew how things should be.

She knew of the physical aspects of marriage not from actual experience but from pieces of conversation she heard from friends or from what she had gleaned through reading.

Crandle had never touched her other than to drop a friendly kiss on her forehead. Her late husband, though much older than she, was not hard to look upon. It galled her to know that he had never intended their marriage to be a real one. Whether he did not wish to consummate their vows or was unable to, she never knew. It was not a subject they ever discussed.

Miranda sighed. "No, Bea. Puddings were definitely not a favorite of Crandle's. And so I do look forward to having some."

Chapter Four

*E*van lounged against cushions that had been placed on the heavy carpet under the canopy. The cool breeze chilled his neck, tempting him to put on his coat. Instead, he stretched out his legs before him and watched Miranda's approach. She walked toward him, her arm linked with Lady Rothwell's. Miranda's steps were purposeful, as if she needed to concentrate on the simple task.

Her eyes tried to give nothing away, but she looked flustered. His heart skipped a beat when her stormy hazel gaze locked onto his and her eyes darkened with anger. She looked quite incredible when she was angry.

He still felt the warmth of holding her in his arms. That simple act had wreaked havoc with his senses, but in the end, he had managed to remain in control. He believed that if he showed her what she had carelessly tossed aside, what she made them both miss, then perhaps through such punishing of her, he might wash away some of the bitterness he carried with him. It would be sweet torment of a purely physical kind.

He had to own that he had not expected to feel so strong an attraction. Needing to leave his coat off to cool his heated body should be alarm enough to him that he was playing with fire. But this time, he swore, he'd not be the one to be burned.

Seven years ago when he had first met Miranda, he had been hit with the reaction George Clasby said he longed to experience. Evan had fallen head over heels in love with Miranda at first sight. He flirted with Miranda and courted her, feeling as if he had fallen under some sort of spell. The madness he felt for her had nearly suffocated him. He had to have her, had to marry her and love her for always. And she had agreed to become his wife.

Until she married the Earl of Crandle.

Bitterness rose again like bile in his throat, and he reached for a glass of ale to wash it away. He had come here to woo Artemis Rothwell. With her, his life would remain calm, composed, and settled. He had maintained this balance these last seven years. He would continue this course until the day he died. There would be no madness, no desperation, and no hotheaded, jealous rages. With Artemis Rothwell, he could anticipate a peaceful relationship in rustic bliss. If he could rid himself of Miranda's effect on him while he taught her a lesson, then so much the better. His hurt might finally be put to rest.

"Miranda." Lady Rothwell handed her a plate. "A healthy portion of plum pudding saved for all of us!"

"Thank goodness," Miranda said, with mock melodrama. "I do not know what I should have done if Rothwell had eaten it all."

Evan found himself smiling at her reaction. She looked younger when she was lighthearted.

"Yes, especially after Crandle kept you away from such pleasures," Lady Rothwell teased.

He saw the smile upon Miranda's face stiffen and

freeze. Her eyes betrayed her discomfort, regardless of her attempt to laugh at Lady Rothwell's harmless comment. Lady Rothwell, whose back was turned, had no idea that she had said something amiss.

But Evan had.

He watched as Miranda carefully took her plate of pudding and sat down upon a plump cushion. She played with her spoon, swirling it about her plate, until finally she took a bite of the rich dessert. She looked up, and their eyes met. The pain and guilt he read in her gaze startled him. She quickly looked away, and he wondered what had caused her distress.

"Lord Ashbourne." Artemis Rothwell plopped down next to him, capturing his attention. Her face was alight with eagerness.

"Miss Rothwell?" he asked with amusement.

"After our tour of Ashby Castle, would you care to race back to Rothwell Park?"

He rubbed his chin. "That would depend upon what your father has to say."

"He will race with us, of course." She sounded almost indignant, as if she would never dream of leaving her father behind.

"Very well, then, a race we shall have."

She clapped her hands together with glee. She looked very young indeed. He caught Miranda watching them. "What of you, Lady Crandle? Will you race with us?" he asked. But her haughtiness was firmly back in place. He could not help but wish it gone.

He wanted to see her abandon the reserve she wore like armor and give over to pure enjoyment, if only for the chance to see her once again as she was when they had first met. The thought that the last

seven years had not been kind ones for her did not
sit well with him, even though he cursed the pain
she had caused him.

She sat straighter. "I thank you, but no, I do not
believe I shall race this time."

"Oh, do consider it, Miranda," Miss Rothwell said.
"It will be such fun."

Evan noticed that Miranda's smile softened when
she looked upon the younger girl. "I shall indeed
consider it and give you my answer after our tour."

Miss Rothwell was satisfied and turned her attention to him. The breeze played with the stray locks
that had escaped from her upswept hairstyle. "Tell
me, Lord Ashbourne," she said, "after you ride your
grey, which one of my father's horses interests you?"

Evan finally slipped on his coat. The air was cool.
He pulled at the modest lace cuffs of his lawn shirt so
that they peeped out from his coat sleeves. "I don't
quite know. Elias is a wonderful horse with immense
spirit. I may just ride him the entire time, if he holds
up well. I brought the young gelding I recently purchased from your Papa as well. He's a bit green, but
he needs to start learning the ropes in the field."

"We have one even better than your Elias," she
said. "I would be happy to show him to you."

The opportunity to spend some time alone with
her had presented itself. He liked what he knew of
her thus far. Artemis Rothwell was a kind young
lady with a vigorous interest in life, and yet she appeared also to be a peaceful person. She was content
in the country. He rather doubted Miss Rothwell
would pine for London. Even so, he needed to know
her better before he approached her papa for permission to pay his addresses.

"Miss Rothwell," he said, "I would be glad to see

this magnificent hunter you boast of. Perhaps you might accompany me on a ride to test his mettle?"

Anticipation shone from her eyes. "I should like that above all things."

The meal was made ready and the food served alfresco, with each person making do without tables or chairs. Evan thoroughly enjoyed his meal. He ate well, even though he had sampled the pudding first, as had everyone else. He preferred the easy, informal atmosphere the Rothwells encouraged to the stiff formality of most noble gatherings. Even George Clasby, an extremely proper gentleman, seemed comfortable supping on pieces of cheese and watercress sandwiches without the display of crystal and polished silver.

Miranda, on the other hand, appeared almost ill at ease with the informal picnic. She sat with her back ramrod straight throughout the entire meal. She looked almost afraid to relax and enjoy herself. She chatted with Lady Rothwell, who must be well accustomed to Miranda's demeanor.

The two seemed ill-matched to be such close friends. Lady Rothwell was warm, with an easy manner that encouraged one and all to be comfortable in her presence. Miranda had turned into a snobbish high society woman. Evan realized that he had not heard her truly laugh since he had arrived. That bothered him more than he cared to admit.

As the servants cleared away the remaining dishes of food, Evan made his way to ready his horse. Clasby joined him.

"Are you going to tell me what there is between you and Lady Crandle?" Clasby asked.

Evan felt the hairs on the back of his neck stand up. "What do you mean?"

"You have been watching her throughout our picnic. I thought it was the Rothwell chit you planned to court."

"Do not say that you have an interest in Lady Crandle." Evan was appalled at the surge of jealousy that seared his insides.

"What is she to you?" Clasby asked with a cheeky grin.

"Nothing," Evan lied.

Clasby's gaze narrowed.

Evan knew that look. Clasby saw right through him. "We met a long time ago," he explained.

Realization suddenly dawned on his friend's face. "Do not say that Lady Crandle is the reason you have sworn never again to love."

Evan shook his head as he tightened the girth of his horse's saddle. "I will say nothing of the kind."

"What if I was interested in a mere dalliance? She is a beautiful woman and a widow besides," Clasby said.

Evan snapped the leather tight before turning to his friend. "Perhaps that is what I had in mind. To sow a few wild oats before I wed."

Miranda trudged along the path, trying to look interested in the history lesson the groundskeeper gave them. She was cold, tired, and sore from riding. She did not belong in the country, not any more. In the country, people were often too open. There was nowhere for her to hide. At least in town she could pretend to be happy. She had done so for years.

Seeing Evan brought all the remorse she had been trying to bury back to the forefront of her emotions. She felt raw and exposed, even though no one really knew.

No one but Evan.

He kept looking at her as if there was something wrong with her. She feared that he could see right through her, slicing open her heart and soul for his inspection. When he had held her, even if only for a brief moment, it had burned her flesh with longing. How could he possibly know that she yearned to be held by him?

"Beautiful bushes," Mr. Clasby was at her side.

"If you like bushes," she answered.

"You do not?" he asked, with mock disdain.

"I have never given them much thought," she answered. Mr. Clasby was a gentleman, but she knew the predatory look of a rake. Widows made easy prey, and Miranda had become adept at steering clear of gentlemen looking for mistresses.

"I remember seeing you in town," Mr. Clasby said.

"Oh?" She knew of Mr. Clasby but had never met him before. He had earned a reputation for pleasing the ladies. She had heard many whispers about him.

She did not veer far from her own small circle of friends in town. They were not true friends like Beatrice or even Artemis. They were social friends who appreciated her only because she was the wife of an earl with impeccable behavior, breeding, and looks.

"They have a name for you, did you realize that?" Clasby asked.

"No, and I cannot imagine what it might be." She braced herself for the pet name the *ton* had given her.

"The Portrait of Beauty."

She nearly grimaced. Such a name was laced with double meanings. Crandle was well known for his collection of art. Did the *ton* know that she had merely been part of his collection? It was demeaning to realize that they might have suspected the emptiness of her marriage. It might also explain the bold propositions she had received over the years.

"Not exactly a name that inspires pride," she murmured.

"I disagree," Mr. Clasby said, with feeling. "Your beauty, Lady Crandle, is indeed timeless."

She refrained from sighing. She had been given these compliments before. "Thank you."

"—Even if Ashbourne disagrees with such a name."

She felt her spine stiffen. She wondered what Evan might have said on the matter. Even so, she needed to change the subject. "How long have you known Lord Ashbourne?"

"His land borders mine. We met while hunting grouse soon after he came into the title. We often hunt together when I am at home in Derbyshire."

"I see," she said. They had fallen behind the others, and she did not wish to be alone with him for any length of time. "Perhaps we should walk faster, Mr. Clasby, and catch up with the tour."

"Of course." He looked at her a moment longer than necessary, but he increased his pace.

She wondered what on earth he could be thinking. She did not care for his scrutiny; it seemed he had considerable depth of character beneath his devil-may-care manner.

"Ashbourne has never accompanied me to London. I always found that odd. He never wanted anything to do with the Season or sessions in Parliament. Now that he wishes to set up his nursery, you would think London the perfect place for him. But he will have none of it."

Miranda nearly stopped in her tracks. She felt as if the wind had been knocked out of her. It was true;

Evan was looking for a wife! Miranda cleared her throat, hoping her voice sounded even. "Has Lord Ashbourne made his choice, then?"

"He has," Mr. Clasby said. "He is interested in Miss Rothwell."

Miranda closed her eyes. He was too old for her! "I see," she said, with forced indifference. "Rothwell will no doubt be pleased."

Miranda knew that Lord Rothwell had found a kindred spirit in Evan Langley, Earl of Ashbourne. Both men were excessively fond of riding and other sporting pursuits. Which meant that Artemis would no doubt be drawn to him, too. If Evan aimed to woo her, she would be smitten before the end of the week.

Mr. Clasby gingerly touched her shoulder. "Are you all right?" he asked with real concern.

"Completely." She sloughed off his arm and walked forward, only to halt. " 'Tis merely a slight cramp in my foot," she said quickly. She stooped down to rub the back of her calf. "There, that it is much better."

"Might I be of assistance," Mr. Clasby said, as he bent down onto his haunches. "I am somewhat of an expert at curing such ailments."

Miranda frowned at his bold offer. "I am sure that you are, but I must decline. Thank you."

"As you wish." He stood with a Gallic shrug and offered her his arm.

They walked the rest of the way in silence, and Miranda let herself gaze at the massive ruins before them. The golden stone walls left standing despite several sieges filled the landscape with romance. Miranda could almost see ladies-in-waiting watching the knights jousting in the field.

"A beautiful heap," Mr. Clasby said, with a tone of wonder in his voice. "It is said that Mary Queen of Scots stayed here on two occasions."

"Did she? I was thinking how lovely it must have been with lords and ladies of old and richly garbed priests keeping the faith."

Mr. Clasby made a face.

"What have I said?" Miranda asked with a slight smile.

"I was enjoying your vision until you mentioned the clergy."

"Not a man of religious beliefs?" Miranda found herself curious.

"That is a good way of putting it," Mr. Clasby said. "Come, let us envision instead the Norman knights gathering in the field for a tournament."

They came within sight of the others, and Miranda's fairy-tale vision was shattered. Evan escorted Artemis, and the two were laughing. Artemis had dared Evan to climb the Hastings Tower, and he appeared all too ready to oblige her. Miranda knew Mr. Clasby's words were most probably true, but the weight of them still hit her hard.

Evan noticed Clasby paying close attention to Miranda as he stood on the upper reaches of Hastings Tower. Artemis leaned from an open window pointing out any number of sights, but his gaze was riveted instead upon his friend with Miranda.

He had spotted them almost immediately. Miranda looked uncomfortable, but then he did not know when she had ever looked comfortable since he had arrived. He wondered if perhaps Clasby was planning to go ahead and attempt a dalliance. If so, was Miranda willing? The thought did not sit well with him, and he wanted to kick himself for caring. Why should it matter what Miranda did, or whom she chose to do it with!

He had hoped by declaring his own intent to pursue a dalliance with Miranda that Clasby would keep his distance. But then, Clasby might have taken it as a challenge of sorts, to see who would be first to coax the fair Lady Crandle into offering up her luscious lips for a passionate kiss.

Evan knew those lips well. He had tasted their sweetness years ago, and the memory still lingered in the recesses of his mind. Would they be as sweet as he had remembered them to be? He'd be hanged if he'd let Clasby find out.

"A penny for your thoughts, Lord Ashbourne?" Artemis asked him.

He forced his thoughts to cool as he turned smiling eyes upon the gentle giantess he had come to woo. He must make progress before the droves of young men arrived to steal away his chance. "I was considering how best to beat you in our race," he said.

Artemis smiled, showing a perfect set of even white teeth. "Do not be too flippant about it, my lord. I am an excellent rider. I will give you strong competition."

"Spoken like a true Rothwell," he said.

"Aye, she is that!" Lord Rothwell joined them in the tower. "So, who will race with us?"

Evan was surprised to hear Miranda's voice as she climbed up the tower stairs. "I think I shall join in your race."

Artemis nearly jumped up and down. "How wonderful!"

"And if Miranda is to join in, then I shall also," Lady Rothwell added.

"I won't be left out," Clasby said with a smile. He was the last to join them high in the tower.

"It is settled. We shall leave in one half hour. We shall start out slowly to warm up, and then, once we clear the castle's land, it is a race to the end at Rothwell Park."

"Father, what shall the winner receive?" Artemis asked.

"A kiss!" Rothwell announced, with a wink toward his wife. "The winner shall claim a kiss from whomever they choose!"

Evan laughed, as did the rest of the group, but Miranda looked worried. Evan considered that if he won, he might enjoy claiming his kiss from her but then thought better of it. He'd be mortified if he came even close to losing control in public.

"To the horses, then, in half of an hour," Artemis agreed, as she walked off with Lady Rothwell and Miranda to ready themselves for the seven-mile race back to Rothwell Park.

Evan mounted his horse. The dappled gray hunter danced about, as if sensing the excitement to come. "Easy now, boy. We will be off in a moment," he murmured.

"He's quite ready to go." Miranda's mare kept her distance from the now stomping stallion.

"Are you?" he asked, as the others gathered around. They'd have a proper start called by one of the servants.

"I shall find out soon enough," she answered with a reluctant smile. A hint of the old Miranda peeked through, reminding Evan how charming she could be.

"Are we all present and accounted for?" Lord Rothwell asked as he looked around. "Very well,

Sams," he said to the servant. "On your call, we shall start our race."

Evan's muscles involuntarily tensed in preparation for action. Although the race was merely for amusement, he still felt the surge of desire to win. He cast a quick glance at Artemis Rothwell. Did the girl boast justifiably of her equestrian prowess? She looked as ready for flight as her mare. He would have expected her to ride one of her father's prized hunters, but then this had been only a recreational outing.

Sams shouted the start, and they urged their mounts forward. Artemis and her father took the lead immediately. Evan felt he should remain close to Lady Rothwell and Miranda in case they ran into any trouble and held his hunter back.

"Go on, Lord Ashbourne," Lady Rothwell chided him. "You needn't play nursemaid to either of us. We know what we are about, and if need be, we shall slow down."

"Yes, Ashbourne, do stretch that magnificent animal's legs. I shall make sure the ladies come to no harm," Clasby assured him.

He narrowed his eyes at Clasby who merely smiled. He then looked at Miranda, who was flushed from the exertion but looked exhilarated nonetheless. He nodded in her direction before tightening his legs to urge Elias into a gallop. He had to own he wanted a firsthand look at just how well Miss Rothwell rode.

In no time, he caught up to Rothwell and his daughter, but he could not maintain a full gallop and eventually dropped Elias back into a steady canter. In a moment, Artemis Rothwell's mare pounded past him. With a wave of her hand, she left him and her father literally in the dust. Her mare showed no signs of letting up.

"She's aiming to win," Rothwell called out.

"Aye." Evan looked back to see that Clasby and the ladies had fallen far behind. He looked back at Rothwell, who read his mind. Second place had yet to be determined, and Evan wanted to beat his host. They urged their mounts faster, each struggling to overtake the other.

When they finally galloped into the stable yard, Miss Rothwell had already dismounted. She stood beaming with pride. "What took you so long?" she called out, with a saucy grin.

Evan beat out Rothwell by the length of his stallion's neck. He slowed his mount to a stop and slid from the saddle. He handed the reins to a groom, who'd ride the horse until it had cooled down. "Your mare is remarkably fast," he said breathlessly.

"She is faster than any of my father's horses."

Rothwell was right behind him, slapping him on the back. "She is that. Artemis has trained that mare since it was born. They think and move as one."

"Now you tell me. Had I no chance at all?" Evan asked, when he had caught his breath.

"Of course you did. The hunters are bred for strength as well as speed, in order to endure a long hunt. My mare has only roamed these roads and trails. She had the advantage of knowing the way well."

"A gracious winner." Evan bowed.

When Lady Rothwell, Miranda, and Clasby arrived some minutes later, they had not moved from the stable yard.

"Now that all have arrived," Miss Rothwell announced, "I shall claim my prize." She hesitated slightly, her cheeks red. "I demand a kiss from the gentleman who won second place. Lord Ashbourne, I believe that is you."

Evan felt completely uncomfortable. Artemis Rothwell did not hold out her hand, as a gently bred young miss should. Instead, she puckered up her lips and tilted her head back. He looked nervously to her father for guidance.

"Go ahead, Ashbourne." He gave Evan a little push. "I give you leave to kiss my daughter respectfully for her victory."

Evan felt his cheeks reddening. He stepped close to Miss Rothwell, who had closed her eyes, and gingerly placed his lips upon her own for the briefest of kisses. He opened his eyes and found himself looking directly into hers. She looked surprised and almost disappointed. He drew back from her, embarrassed, even though everyone cheered with good humor.

Everyone except Miranda.

She did not appear to be in the least pleased. She remained on her horse after the others had dismounted.

"I think I shall ride directly into the stable," Evan overheard Miranda say to Clasby.

Something was wrong. He watched her direct her horse around the corner after assuring Lady Rothwell that all was well. Miss Rothwell and her mother headed for the main house, and Rothwell and Clasby followed the ladies.

Evan followed Miranda.

Chapter Five

*M*iranda felt an odd sense of betrayal. Evan had kissed Artemis while Beatrice and Rothwell looked on with approval. What Mr. Clasby had said at Ashby de la Zouch was not only true but also encouraged. How could Beatrice think Evan good for a daughter newly turned nineteen! The match might make perfect sense, and yet Miranda could not warm to it. In fact, she thought it a terrible idea.

Carefully she urged the mare she rode into the stables. The sweet smell of hay and horse assaulted her nose. It was not an unpleasant odor, simply an unfamiliar one.

She had spent little time in or near stables over the course of her life. When she was growing up, her parents had had their horses made ready and brought round to the drive by grooms. Crandle did not permit her to set foot inside a stable, as he considered it beneath her. And so she entered the Rothwell stable as if it were a new world that awaited her. It was a world where Evan, and even Artemis, moved about freely with complete comfort.

She looked around for a groom to help her dismount, but there was no one in sight. The mare she rode continued to move forward into the stall that must have been hers. The horse lowered her head and began munching on a pile of fresh hay.

Miranda shifted in her saddle. She experienced severe soreness. "Oh Lud," she whispered. How was she to dismount without falling in a heap on the stable floor? Her right foot had fallen completely asleep.

"Did your husband know you used such language, Lady Crandle?" Evan asked from behind her.

She closed her eyes and bit her lip to keep from letting out a real indecency. His constant comments regarding her late husband, no matter how correct, irritated her. But she was in a coil, and she needed help. "If you please," she said through gritted teeth—she hurt like the very devil—"I do need your assistance."

"I noticed that you did not dismount in the yard."

"I did not wish to make a spectacle of myself." She nearly groaned as she moved. "I should be better at this than I am."

"Dear Miranda, always striving for perfection."

His sarcasm raked against her already raw feelings. "You do not know a thing about me, Evan Langley," she snapped, letting him get the better of her composure.

She saw him smile with satisfaction. He had baited her into anger, and she had given in too easily. "It's Ashbourne now," he reminded her.

She refrained from rolling her eyes. "Where is the groom?" she asked.

"He is investigating the main stables that will be used for the hunt. He took a couple of the boys with him. I do not know where the rest have gone. Perhaps they are at luncheon." Evan reached his arms up toward her.

Miranda experienced a shiver that ran down her spine. The temptation to be in those arms again was nearly overwhelming, despite her aching body. She hesitated slightly before finally leaning into him. She felt his strength as he practically lifted her from the saddle. He did not release her when her feet touched the ground because her knees gave way and she sank into his chest. "This is absurd," she complained, when she found it difficult to stand. Her right foot still tingled as if she stepped on shards of broken glass, but at least feeling had returned. She stamped on it three times.

"Stretch it out," he said with a grin. "Here, I will hold on to you."

She glared at him, but did as he bade. She bent low in an attempt to stretch out her trembling legs. She felt unsteady as she took slow, painful steps out of the stall.

"Here." Evan suddenly swept her up and into his arms. "It will take all day for you to reach the main house at this rate."

Miranda gasped and sputtered with indignation as he settled her more comfortably. The warmth of him radiating into her body was too much. The temptation to wrap her arms about his neck nearly swamped her. "Evan, you lobcock, put me down this instant."

He stopped and smiled, his dimples teasing her. "I will not."

"Oh!" She thrashed.

"Miranda, be still." His eyes turned to a dark gray, but his look was more serious than amorous. "There is no harm in carrying you inside."

She wrenched free from his arms. She was not about to be carried, by him of all people, into the house. She was on her feet for only a moment before she lost her balance and fell backwards into the stall, landing in a pile of hay.

She lay there, breathing harder than her exertion called for. She felt like a fool. She looked up to see that every trace of humor had left Evan's face. His gaze traveled the length of her.

She felt trapped by his bold inspection like a butterfly that had been pinned on a board. Her breathing did not ease; it came harder and more ragged.

"You are so beautiful," he whispered and looked surprised at having said it aloud.

"You have no right to say such a thing," she said in a strangled small voice.

He knelt beside her. "Do I not?"

She scrambled to a more respectable sitting position and hurried to cover her ankles, which had been revealed to his view. "Evan," she sighed, suddenly weary of him, "what do you want of me?"

"I do not know," he said. His eyes took on a troubled look as he reached out and caressed her cheek with the palm of his hand. The gentleness of his touch took her breath away and left her feeling weak and wanting.

"Perhaps this." He leaned toward her. His lips touched hers only briefly, and then he pulled back as if reconsidering his actions.

Not so Miranda. She reached up and pulled his head down, pressing her lips against his. She heard him groan, as if giving in to her.

With a strangled gasp, she opened to him, and her body felt as if it had burst into flame as he explored her mouth with his tongue. Fire burned within her at the same time as a sorrow buried deep inside her soul broke loose. Tears stung her eyelids, and she felt as if she were drowning.

Pushing at him, she nearly choked on the emotions overwhelming her. "Stop it," she panted. "Evan, please, stop." She pulled away from him and drew back into the hay.

Evan sat on his haunches, his hair disheveled, as was his cravat. She must have disarranged them both. His breathing was uneven, and he looked confused. "Miranda—" he started.

"Please, just go," she managed around the lump in her throat. She would not let him see her cry, nor did she wish to embarrass herself further. She wanted him so badly it hurt. She feared that if he did not leave, she would have no willpower to stop him if he should kiss her again.

"No. I'll not leave you out here when you can barely walk." The softness in his eyes undid her resolve.

She wanted more than anything to throw herself back into his arms and let him sweep her away with kisses, but she could not delude herself. There were years of bitterness and remorse between them.

Evan had come to court another. He had come to Rothwell Park with the intent of marrying Artemis. One kiss did not change that fact. It made matters still worse, and Miranda was riddled with guilt.

"Very well," she said. It would not do to remain in the stable. Once alone, she very much feared she would fall apart completely. She struggled for composure. She tipped her head back and cast Evan the frostiest look of condescension she could muster. She reached up her hands, and he pulled her to her feet. "Evan, please do let me walk on my own."

He nodded and offered his arm.

Her steps were slow and tentative, but as she forced herself to put one foot in front of the other, stretching her legs as she went, she felt them begin to strengthen. Evan remained silent next to her, and for that she was grateful.

She did not trust herself to speak because of the swell of emotion in her throat that longed for release. She dared not discuss what had transpired between them in the stable. She had the frightening feeling that she just might beg for another kiss, should they reflect upon it.

She glanced at Evan. He looked even less inclined to examine it. Perhaps it was best to simply forget it.

But what did Evan's immediate response to her kiss mean for Artemis? It was not at all the thing for a man to kiss the lady he courted playfully while her parents looked on with smiles and then dissolve into heated passion while kissing another only moments later. Miranda could not help but wonder if she should somehow intervene. But was it her place to do so if Beatrice and Rothwell both approved of Evan for their daughter?

If she did interfere, what would her true motives be? She had a mind to capture Evan for herself—at least her body wanted him. She would never dream of breaking Artemis' heart. She would not do that for the world. If she stole Evan away from Artemis, she could crush a young lady's aspirations and lose a longtime friendship with Beatrice.

She glanced at Evan, who looked more distant than ever. He had complete control over his expression. The stiffness of his arm and the tension she felt in him were the only clues that something was amiss. She breathed a sigh of relief when they finally entered the main hall.

Beatrice met them with a look of concern. "Miranda, dearest, I must beg your pardon. You are not used to riding so hard."

"Do not concern yourself, Bea. The decision to race was mine," Miranda said.

"Lady Crandle." Evan bowed. "I leave you in the good hands of our hostess."

"Thank you, Ashbourne." Miranda understood Evan's retreat into formality. It was something she did often.

Once Evan had walked down the hall, Beatrice turned to her and asked. "Is everything all right?"

Miranda would not look her friend in the eye. She did not wish to give anything away. "Fine, my dear, I am simply embarrassingly sore."

Beatrice narrowed her gaze but did not push the issue. "A hot bath will be just the thing! Come, I will help you to your rooms."

Miranda followed, immensely relieved that Beatrice asked her nothing more.

Evan made his way to the empty drawing room. A cheery fire crackled and hissed in the grate, beckoning him to step closer. He felt suddenly cold. He pulled a chair near and dropped into it with a disgusted grunt. He'd been a fool to think he could kiss Miranda lightly. Blast and tarnation! It was still there. The hunger he once felt for her burned anew inside his breast. He wanted her still.

And she wanted him.

He had almost come out unscathed after searing his lips only briefly against hers. But then she had pulled him down and kissed him, and he had let himself succumb completely in the taste of her.

He had warned Clasby that he wanted a dalliance

with her in order to chase him away from the same idea. Evan had not realized how strong that intent would become. He wanted Miranda. But how could he pursue anything further with her when they were guests in the home of the lady he had come to court?

He stood up and walked across the room to pour a bit of brandy from the decanters lined up against the far wall. He drained his glass with one gulp, but it did no good. The calming effects of spirits were lost to him. He felt more agitated than ever.

He need only make it through the week and then he'd be gone. With luck, he'd have Lord Rothwell's blessing to marry his daughter and her acceptance by the end of the week as well. He must forget about Miranda. She had only brought him pain.

Miranda lay in a steaming tub of luxuriously fragrant water. The steamy heat that drew perspiration from her brow hid the tears streaming uncontrollably down her face. What on earth was she to do? She longed for Evan, and her heart ached terribly. For seven years she had buried her pain and regret. She had stifled all her feelings when she walked sacrificially into a loveless marriage with Lord Crandle for the sake of her family's estate. She knew after only a year that the sacrifice had not been worth the cost. She had lost something very precious, and now that loss reared its head, demanding its due.

Another sob threatened to choke her, but she forced it into submission. She could not wallow in self-pity about what might have been. It hurt too much. The water swirled as she stood, wrapping herself in a soft warm robe, just as Beatrice knocked on the door of her dressing room. "Come in," she called out.

"How are you feeling?" Beatrice asked.

"Much restored, I thank you."

"Come and sit with me a moment."

Miranda nodded and followed Beatrice into the small sitting room overlooking the courtyard. Miranda sat quietly while Beatrice traced the design of the sofa with her finger. Miranda knew Beatrice was gathering her thoughts for a serious discussion. She also knew it had to do with Evan.

"Is everything as it should be between you and Lord Ashbourne?" Beatrice finally asked.

Miranda closed her eyes. What could she say? "Bea—" she started.

Beatrice held up her hand to stop any further words. "It is not my business to pry, but since we have hopes of Lord Ashbourne for Artemis, I wanted to ask what you thought of him. You appear uncomfortable around him. I wanted to ask you if I should be concerned for Artemis' sake."

Miranda let out the breath she'd been holding. "Ashbourne, I am sure, is a fine man."

"But you knew him before meeting him here, is that not so?"

Miranda was not about to lie to her friend, but she could not tell her about that afternoon's kiss in the stables. Besides, Miranda had no idea what effect their shared kiss would have on their future relations. It may have been a fleeting moment of weakness and nothing more. "I met Lord Ashbourne when I made my bows in London. He was simply Mr. Langley then."

"Just after I had married Rothwell." Beatrice tucked her feet up underneath her gown. She leaned back in anticipation of a story.

"Yes."

Realization dawned on Beatrice's face. "Oh, Miranda, do not tell me Ashbourne is the man you nearly married!"

Miranda winced. She had never told Beatrice how deep her feelings were for Evan. No one, with the exception of perhaps her father, knew just how deeply in love with Evan she had fallen in the two short months of her Season. Neither had she ever told Beatrice why she had chosen to marry Crandle. She did not wish to dishonor her father with such a tale.

Even so, Beatrice had been her governess, and being thus in the employ of her father, no doubt she had gleaned some of the financial concerns affecting her father's estate. Miranda had married Crandle for the security he bestowed upon her family. Evan had offered neither wealth nor security at a time when she needed both.

"It was a long time ago, Bea," Miranda said. Another truth. After seven years, she should have lost her feelings for Evan completely.

"Yes, but how do you feel about him now?"

That was a question she had no answer for. "I do not know. I barely know him now." And that, too, was indeed the truth.

"Oh, dear." Beatrice got to her feet, obviously disturbed by this revelation.

Miranda also stood, wringing her hands as she watched her friend closely. "Beatrice, Ashbourne shows respectable interest in Artemis. Do you know if she favors him?" Miranda waited with bated breath for the answer.

"You know how it is to be young and headstrong.

She will not tell me a thing! Rothwell definitely favors him. He knows him well and trusts him completely."

"Well, then, there you are," Miranda said. It was a weak response.

Beatrice reached out and grasped Miranda's hands to still them. "But what do you think?"

"Truly? I think Ashbourne too old for her."

Beatrice bit her lower lip as she considered this.

"And Artemis deserves a love match," Miranda added.

"Yes, but that could come in time. Look at Rothwell and me."

"Look at Crandle and me," Miranda said, with meaning.

"But Ashbourne is nothing like Crandle," Beatrice said.

Miranda knew Beatrice did not understand. Miranda feared that Ashbourne's motives for pursuing Artemis had little to do with any depth of affection. They were no better than Crandle's, really. He'd not have kissed her today in the stables had he cared for Artemis. That truth had been stewing in her thoughts ever since she'd returned to the house.

How could she save Artemis from a fate that she herself had suffered in a marriage of convenience if the girl was determined to have Ashbourne as husband? And still more troubling was the fact that Beatrice and Rothwell approved of the match.

"Well," Beatrice started. "Nothing is decided, and the other guests have yet to arrive. I must attend to Cook and ensure we are prepared for this evening's supper." Beatrice placed her hands on Miranda's shoulders. "Please keep a watchful eye upon Artemis. She admires you so, and I know she will heed your counsel, even if she will not abide by that of her own parents."

Miranda felt a swell of emotion rise in her chest. "I want only what is best for her, you know."

Beatrice hugged her. "I know you do, dear. We all do." With a tight squeeze, she let her go and left the room.

Miranda sat back down upon the sofa, falling backwards to lie down facing the ceiling. She placed her fingers against her temples in an attempt to ease the dull ache. What if Evan was indeed the best thing for Artemis? What then? After kissing him, Miranda wondered if she could give Evan up a second time.

Regardless, for Artemis' sake, she could not let the kiss she had shared with Evan go by without some explanation from him. She needed to find out what Evan wanted and why. She only hoped that while she tried to save Artemis from heartbreak, she did not plunge herself into it instead.

The day had darkened into evening, and candlelight shone from every sconce at Rothwell Park. A festive mood enlivened the air, and laughter could be heard coming from the larger, more formal drawing room that had been opened for the house party. Several guests had arrived late in the afternoon, so dinner had been delayed.

The invited guests, higher in estate than in previous years, mingled easily in the room, draped in their finest silks and knee breeches. Jewels glittered and winked from the ladies' necks and ears. Men wore stickpins of gold and gemstones tucked in the snowy folds of impeccable linen cravats.

Miranda went immediately to Beatrice's side. "Bea, you look very fine indeed. Is everything as it should be?" she asked.

"It's perfect," Beatrice answered. "Lord Cole has been installed in the yellow suite, and the Waterton-Smythes have found their missing luggage."

Miranda gave her friend's hand a squeeze. "You are doing exceedingly well. You will no doubt be hailed as a premier hostess. This gathering rivals any in London. From now on you will be besieged with visitors."

"Oh dear, do not tell Rothwell. He will have my hide," she said with mock alarm, but Miranda saw that Beatrice beamed with pride. She was well on her way to proving herself completely competent in entertaining some of the highest sticklers. The Waterton-Smythes were a lofty family indeed.

Beatrice's previous role as a governess appeared to be forgotten and put firmly in the past. It should not have mattered in any case since Beatrice was of noble birth and lineage, even if once she had been poor.

Rothwell strutted about the room, clearly enjoying the chance to boast about the portion of his lands being used for the hunt. Miranda mingled with the arriving guests, ignoring their surprise at finding her in the country.

Artemis finally entered on the arm of Lord Ashbourne. Miranda noted the proprietary gleam in Evan's eye, and her hopes sank. His entry made a quiet statement to the young men present that he was a serious contender for Miss Rothwell's favor.

Dressed in a simple gown of dull gold silk, Artemis looked much more mature than the other young women, who were garbed in insipid white lace and ruffles. Miranda smiled. Although not a beauty and nowhere near delicate, Artemis Rothwell was a handsome young woman whose presence demanded attention. Miranda was pleased that Artemis held her head high, even when the two Waterton-Smythe sisters whispered behind their fans.

Beatrice was trapped by a grand matron of significant social standing, and Rothwell laughed with several men in the far corner of the room. Miranda needed to make introductions for Artemis where she could before dinner. She made her way to Evan and Artemis, where they stood talking to Mr. Clasby and Miss Whitlow, a very pretty young lady of the same years as Artemis.

Miranda made a gentle entry into the foursome. "Good evening, Miss Whitlow, Mr. Clasby." Miranda bowed to them, then turned to Evan. "Ashbourne, I must beg Miss Rothwell's company so that I may make the rounds with her."

"Good evening, Lady Crandle," Evan bowed stiffly. "Of course." Evan patted Artemis' hand before dropping his arm. Miranda detected his reluctance. Evan's parting glance toward Artemis Rothwell was not one of affection so much as regret that he must be parted from her company, much as an owner of a fine horse would be sorry to see the beast taken to the stables.

It was a look she had often detected in Crandle's eyes—a look of proud possession.

"Come, Artemis," Miranda said. "I shall formally introduce you to your guests."

She made good on her promise, and Artemis met every guest in that drawing room before dinner was announced. Several young men had looked favorably upon Artemis, but whether it was with admiration of her person or her large dowry was yet to be seen.

They proceeded into the dining room, which was the epitome of formal elegance. Crystal sparkled in the candlelight, and footmen, dressed in Rothwell's livery of burgundy and gold, stood poised against the walls, ready to assist. Miranda was escorted by the boyishly handsome Lord Cole, a wealthy Irish peer. Evan escorted Artemis.

Miranda was seated between Evan and Miss Whitlow. Thankfully Artemis had been placed between two other gentlemen. Miranda was certain that originally Bea had planned to have Artemis sit next to Evan. She wondered if the change in seating arrangements had anything to do with the discussion they had had. Miranda was glad that Artemis would have an opportunity to converse with other young men. But was it for Artemis' sake or her own that Miranda felt such relief? She decided not to dwell upon it too closely as she turned to converse with Miss Whitlow.

Course after course was set before them, and Miranda turned toward Evan. "How is your pheasant?" she asked lamely. She needed to capture his attention, and now was the perfect chance while his conversation with the lady to his right had come to an end.

"My what?" he asked.

"Oh, never mind. Evan, we need to talk about what happened this afternoon."

He looked taken aback by her request. A slight flush of red colored his neck just above his cravat, though otherwise his composure remained steady. "I'd rather not," he said quietly.

"You should have thought of that beforehand," she said.

"Indeed, I should have." He carefully placed a forkful of food into his mouth.

Miranda waited, but Evan remained quiet. Evidently he wished to avoid discussing what had happened. She knew the right thing to do was to confront him. There was too much at stake for her to let the matter drop. The question was when and where.

Evan knew Miranda was frustrated with him. He could feel her annoyance emanating from her like smoke from a snuffed-out candle. He tried to ignore her, hoping to douse the awareness of her he felt. It did no good. He was conscious of her every graceful move. Even as she picked up the blasted silver, the delicate curve of her wrist caught his eye!

Her beauty far outshone that of any woman present. The dark ruby color of her dress made her lips look as lush and kissable as he knew them to be. If she moved just so, he could feel the hem of her dress brush the tops of his feet. His feelings of renewed desire for her nearly drove him to distraction. He'd unleashed a monster today when he kissed her, and now he'd pay for it dearly.

But he certainly wasn't about to talk about it—not with her, not alone. Like a man suddenly caught in the middle of a deep lake, Evan knew he was treading dangerous waters. If he did not watch himself carefully, he'd slip under and drown.

Chapter Six

$\mathcal{M}$iranda waited with the ladies in the drawing room while the men lingered over their port. She anxiously awaited their return to the drawing room so that she might try to confront Evan again.

The Waterton-Smythe sisters alternately played the pianoforte and turned sheet music. The two might have been twins, they resembled one another so closely. Both were blond and blue-eyed with an innocent, youthful appearance that belied their respective ages of twenty and twenty-one. Although they were of impeccable lineage, it was said that their father had fallen on hard times. The two sisters were looking for wealthy men to marry.

"There you are," Artemis said in a huff when she sat down.

"Have you been looking for me?"

"Not very hard, but yes. Mama wanted me to ask you if you knew of any games we might play when the men join us." Artemis fiddled with the fringe on a pillow that rested against the sofa.

"Of course. There are several we might choose from. We could play cards, which would separate us into groups, or we might play a word game all together. I am fond of crambo. And there is always charades."

Artemis made a face. "I do not think Papa would care to play charades."

"No, I cannot quite picture your father acting out a riddle."

The two laughed at the shared joke until Artemis fell silent. Miranda knew there was something on her mind. "What is it, dear?"

"The other young ladies," Artemis said, "will have nothing to do with me."

Miranda's heart twisted. Artemis spoke of the unwed ladies. There could be several reasons, but the one that appeared to be the most probable reason for their coolness and distance was that Artemis had captured the attention of the most eligible gentleman present. Evan, Lord Ashbourne, had title, fortune and looks.

Miranda patted Artemis' hand. "Do not fret. They simply wish Lord Ashbourne had paid them the attention he gave you this evening before dinner. They shall no doubt come around in time."

"Do you think so?" Artemis' voice sounded hopeful.

Miranda was even more strongly convinced that Artemis should have a Season. She needed to spread her wings, make female friends, and flirt with the best gentlemen the *ton* had to offer. Letting her settle for Evan, simply because they had much in common when it came to equestrian interests, was not fair to Artemis. Miranda saw every reason to discourage the match.

"I do." Miranda said, with a smile. Then she asked what she knew she must, "Artemis, what is your opinion of Lord Ashbourne?" She held her breath and braced herself for the answer.

Artemis' smile brightened. "I think him a great gun and a good sport."

"Yes, of course, but what if he paid particular attention to you during this house party?"

Artemis frowned slightly. "That would be all right, I suppose. My father has already shared with me his hopes that Ashbourne will do just that."

Miranda nodded. It was just like Rothwell to tell her such a thing instead of keeping quiet and letting the girl make up her own mind.

"But what are *your* thoughts on the matter." Miranda did not wish to push too hard. As Beatrice said, Artemis had told her nothing. She appeared to be sidestepping the issue with Miranda as well. If Artemis had feelings for Evan, she was not about to discuss them.

"I suppose I could do worse." Again, Artemis traced the fringe upon the pillow. "I am not entirely reconciled to the idea of marriage to anyone at present."

Miranda studied her closely in an effort to detect any deeper feeling Artemis might have for Evan. She came away empty-handed. Artemis Rothwell, though gregarious, easily kept her innermost thoughts and feelings to herself. Miranda detected nothing in her and knew that was exactly as Artemis wished it to be.

Finally, the gentlemen entered the drawing room in various groups and as lone wanderers, and Artemis was quick to leave in search of hunting and horse discussions. Miranda had given Beatrice her suggestions for games to play, leaving the decision entirely up to her. Unoccupied, Miranda wove her way about the room, prudently speaking to every matron present. Each lady spoke glowingly about the Rothwells' hospitality. Beatrice was a success. Artemis would no doubt enjoy an engaging Season, with many doors opened to her.

"Shall we all play a word game?" Beatrice inquired.

Many of the young ladies clapped with glee, while some of the men donned a look of beleaguered tolerance.

"What game shall we choose?" Miss Whitlow asked.

"How about crambo?" Beatrice asked. "We can play in teams of ladies against gentleman or perhaps the older generation against the younger. One player must give a line of verse and each of his teammates must deliver a completely different rhyme to complete it."

"Yes, that sounds marvelous," Lady Waterton-Smythe drawled. "I should think we could play the ladies against the men."

"Very well," Beatrice agreed, and put the plan in motion.

Once the teams were seated in two groups, a representative from each kept a tally of every correct rhyme that earned a point. The team with the most points in an hour would be declared the winner.

After half of an hour, many of the gentlemen made excuses to leave the area of play. In fact, a couple of older gentlemen dropped out completely to start a game of piquet in the corner. Frustrated, the ladies decided to break into groups of their own in order to continue.

Miranda was pleased to notice that the ice appeared to be breaking between Artemis and a couple of young ladies. She looked on with relief as Artemis and Miss Whitlow laughed as they formulated rhymes with their heads together.

Miranda saw Evan slip out of the drawing room and knew her chance to speak privately with him had presented itself. After waiting a few moments, she quietly excused herself without so much as a curiously raised eyebrow.

She slipped down the hall, wondering where Evan might have gone. She checked each room for signs of him, only to find that he had effectively disappeared. She almost did not bother with the breakfast room but peeked her head inside anyway. Through double doors of glass that opened to a small courtyard, she saw a glow of red embers and the telltale smoke of a cheroot. Might it be Evan?

Carefully she made her way through the room and softly opened the doors. The slight click of the latch alerted the gentleman to her presence, and he turned. Light from the distant kitchens illuminated Evan's face. Miranda remained in the shadows, battling her fear. She was almost afraid of what he might say to her about kissing her in the stables. She feared his rejection, and that made her hesitate. She could see him squint in an attempt to see through the darkness to recognize his visitor.

She straightened her shoulders and stepped forward. "Evan," she said quietly, "it is I, Miranda. We must talk."

She heard him let out a resigned sigh of defeat. He brought the cheroot to his lips and inhaled. The end of it gleamed a bright orange-red. She waited while he exhaled a cloud of smoke.

"I did not realize that you smoked cheroots," she said.

"I don't," he answered.

"Then might I ask why you are out here doing just that?" She was amazed that he made no move to put the thing out. He kept puffing away as if determined to ignore her presence.

"You may not."

"Where did you get them? Rothwell does not keep cheroots; Beatrice won't let him."

She heard him snort with contempt as if he'd be hanged before he would let a female make such rules for him.

"Clasby gave me a couple."

She stepped closer, and he nearly blew smoke in her face. When she coughed, he backed away from her. "Really, Evan," she scolded. "Can we please speak privately?"

"We are speaking privately."

"No, we are not. You are quite literally creating a wall of smoke between us."

"Forgive me," he said stiffly. He bowed and dashed the cheroot out upon the ground and crushed it with his foot. "Now, what did you wish to discuss?"

He looked impatient, and incredibly bored, as if she had come to him with something trivial.

She remained quiet a moment while she considered how best to phrase her question. She decided upon a direct course. "Evan, what happened this afternoon in the stables?" she asked. "Why did you kiss me?"

He did not answer straightaway, nor did he look her in the eye. "I do not know," he said quietly. "Perhaps it was simply a thoughtless reversion to what we once were. I beg your pardon, it shall not happen again."

"I see." Miranda felt a twinge of disappointment. It had felt marvelous to be kissed by him. In fact, standing outside in the cool evening air, she was more than tempted to try another kiss, just to see if the feeling would be as strong.

She mentally gave herself a shake. This simply would not do. She knew little of the man Evan had become over the years. She knew only the bitterness towards her that he could not hide. She also knew that he was looking to set up his nursery with her own dearest Artemis.

Evan watched as Miranda bit her lower lip. He'd bet a monkey that she had more on her mind than simply their kiss in the stable. "You wanted to talk, Miranda," he finally said. "So, talk."

He could not help but feel uncomfortable with her. He wanted to get this conversation over and done with. In the future, he decided, he must steer clear of her.

At her continued hesitation, he grew more worried. Surely, she did not feel compromised by him. It was only a kiss. She was a widow, not some green girl. She would not force him into a corner, would she?

He wished he had that blasted cheroot back in his hands, giving him something to focus on besides the beauty of her perfect face. He had taken the cursed things from Clasby hoping to calm his nerves. No such good fortune.

"Honestly, Evan, I do not quite know how to begin," she finally said.

"You could start by telling me why you chose Crandle after you had promised to marry me." For the love of all the saints, why had he said that!

She looked stricken but quickly controlled her features into a look of calm resolve. "Evan, I must hum- bly beg your forgiveness. I was young. Too late, I realized how stupid my choice had been."

He snorted with contempt and then he wanted to kick himself for acting like a boor. The problem was that around Miranda he did not know how to act the polite and polished gentleman. She had always stripped him of that veneer. With her, he was noth- ing more than an ordinary man. And now he reacted like the beef-wit he feared he had become—ruled by his basest emotions and desires. It was lowering and infuriating. He was a master of self-control! He had deliberately lived the last seven years of his life in a predictable, if lonely, routine. But he preferred his almost dull and organized existence; in it he felt safe. In it he could easily control events and his reactions to them.

He did not like what he felt now. Looking at her hurt. He longed to kiss her again but knew such an act would only lead to his ultimate doom. If he pur- sued Miranda, he would lose all the restraint and fortitude that had become a large part of his charac- ter. He would no doubt turn into the raging fool of his youth, ready to give up his very soul for love. And that simply would not do.

As he waited, Miranda paced along the small path in the courtyard. The blooms of the flowering plants had long since withered and fallen. Bulbous red rose- hips dipped and bounced when she brushed past them. "That is not why I have sought you out," she said.

"I imagine not." He wanted to scream at her, ask her if she had any idea how difficult it had been to get over her? No mere apology could wipe away what he had endured. But he held his tongue.

She sat upon a small but sturdy wood bench and looked up at him, a protective gleam in her eye. "Just what are your intentions toward Artemis?" she asked.

He leaned against the tree opposite her. "My intentions are completely honorable, I assure you."

"She is too young for you."

"Her parents do not think so, so why should you?" Evan felt his defenses rise. He did not wish to explain his reasons to her.

"You do not love her." Miranda stood and walked toward him. All traces of her earlier reticence were gone. She looked ready to do battle.

"I do not have to." He came away from the tree to stand directly in front of her. Their feet nearly touched as they stood face to face, glaring at one another.

"Trust me, you most certainly do have to love her. Artemis deserves a love match, and I will see to it that she settles for nothing less."

Evan considered her threat. Who was Miranda to interfere when the girl's own parents considered him a worthy contender for her hand. "You are one to talk," he challenged.

"Exactly so," she said. Her hazel eyes flashed fiercely. "I'll not stand by and let that girl endure my fate."

How dare she compare him to Crandle! "I am nothing like your late husband, Madam," he said as haughtily as he could, considering that he seethed with rage.

She did not back down. "Your motives are the very same."

They stood too close. He noticed that she was breathing heavily, her chest rising and falling due to her agitation. It was enough to turn his anger into something else.

His body reacted to her nearness, and he felt his hands move of their own accord to grip her bare arms and pull her in to his chest. "What do you know of *my* motives?"

"I . . ." Her eyes opened wide, and she looked unsure. But a spark of desire flickered and burned until her gaze was molten.

He stood there, unable even to breathe. He held her close, knowing that if he were to kiss her again, it would ruin everything. He reigned in his senses and let the cool, calming voice of reason pervade his heated blood. He had to let her go—*now!*

He released her and backed away, running a hand through his short dark hair. "Miranda, this is insanity," he finally said. "Let us simply steer clear of one another while we are here, shall we? Let our past stay there. I am trying to build a decent future for myself. You must see to your own as well."

Her resolve faltered, and he glimpsed disappointment in her eyes. She wanted him to kiss her! She wanted him. It did not bear thinking about, and yet visions of loving her seared his mind. He shook his head to clear them.

Artemis Rothwell was a perfectly comfortable wife for him. He wanted none of the madness that Miranda inspired.

"Very well, Evan," Miranda finally said, with a proud lift of her chin. "I shall endeavor to leave you alone while I am here, but do not mistake me. I shall do everything in my power to see to Artemis' happiness." With that, she turned on her heel and returned to the main house.

"But what of yours?" he whispered.

He cursed himself and kicked a rock out of the path. He did not want to care about Miranda's happiness, but for some reason he did. She was not happy, nor had she been since marrying Crandle. Somehow knowing that she too had suffered deeply made it that much harder to remain bitter toward her. He wanted to forgive her, he wanted to . . .

He did not linger to contemplate his innermost wishes. He simply could not have her. His sanity, his sense of the man he had worked so hard to become demanded that he not give in and return to being the hotheaded lunatic he was when he loved her.

It was late, and he was tired. Not used to having his emotions stretched in all directions, he headed for his bedchamber for what he hoped would be a good night's rest.

Miranda did not return to the drawing room. She sent word to Beatrice that she planned to retire for the night because she had a headache. Yet, she could not quite face the solitude of her own chamber after being in Evan's arms.

Nor could she pretend to find sleep after he had so firmly rejected her. Once he had warned her to stay away from him, she felt empty inside. On a whim, she grabbed her pelisse from the anteroom and slipped out the front door before anyone could see her leaving.

The night air had turned cold. They would no doubt see frost in the morning. It was odd that during her entire exchange with Evan, she had not once noticed the chill. She walked about the grounds in an effort to exorcise the effect Evan had over her until she found herself standing in front of the stables. The place of their kiss! Quietly, she opened the door and slipped inside.

The warm smell of horseflesh wafted out to her. The sounds of the fine hunters snuffling and munching hay surrounded her. The soft sounds soothed her, and she stepped further into the darkness. She had not brought a candle or lantern with her, so she groped for the sides of the stalls until her eyes adjusted to the lack of light. The head groomsman's quarters were not far off. Through the opened windows at the far wall of the stables, she could see a warm glow from his rooms.

She sat upon a stool and leaned against the rough wood of a stall door, oblivious to what it might do to the silk gown she wore. This was Evan's world, she mused. While she had buried herself in London society for the past seven years, Evan had turned to outdoor pursuits. She remembered that he tended to run with the Corinthian set when they had met, but still he had fancied himself a polished gentleman about town.

From the comments she had heard from the guests this evening, Evan was hailed as an excellent foxhunter. While Rothwell's reputation for breeding prized hunters was well known in this area, it appeared that few equaled Evan's prowess on the field.

No wonder Rothwell approved of him. Evan made the Rothwell horseflesh look very good indeed. What her father approved of, Artemis did too. Artemis was comfortable in these surroundings, and she would indeed make Evan a "comfortable" wife.

Miranda sighed.

"Comfortable" did not lead to happiness. She supposed in some instances it could. Beatrice and Rothwell were examples of a successful marriage of convenience, although she could not imagine Beatrice being considered comfortable once one got to know her. Beatrice challenged one's thoughts and beliefs for the sheer joy of it.

Artemis deserved more than simply being forgotten in the country to raise a brood of heirs. And that was precisely what Evan had in mind for her, she knew. He had not bothered to find out about the real girl inside. She had watched them closely when they interacted. There were times, at the castle ruins, for example, where Miranda doubted Evan listened to a word of Artemis' excited prattle. It would only get worse, she was sure.

Miranda wished that Evan wanted her instead. She knew she affected him physically, but emotionally he wanted nothing to do with her. Even if she wished to change that, after all these years, could they ever go back and recapture what they once had shared?

A noise caught her attention, and she stood. The stable door opened, and someone entered. She could not tell who it was. She watched as the person bumped along the wall. He carried something in his hands and Miranda wondered why he did not light the lantern. She heard rustling and the sounds of something spilling onto the floor. At a curse uttered in a deep male voice, she decided that she should remain hidden in the shadows.

The man knocked something over that clattered to the ground. He stilled instantly, and she felt her heart beat wildly in her chest. Something was wrong.

The door to the groom's quarters opened. Looking through the opened stable windows, Miranda saw the broad-shouldered groom standing in his open doorway, silhouetted in the light from behind him.

He stood there for an interminable amount of time, and Miranda nearly called to him.

She thought better of it. She could not expose herself to danger, if indeed the man inside the stable was a danger. She stayed quiet. She could not see what the stranger was doing, but he made considerable noise. After some minutes, he slipped quickly out of the stable.

When Miranda's breathing returned to normal, she wondered if perhaps she had let her imagination get the best of her. It might have been nothing. But something felt terribly wrong, and she knew she had to do something about it.

Chapter Seven

*M*iranda paced back and forth in her bedchamber, wringing her hands. She had to tell
someone what she had seen, but whom? She did not
wish to upset Beatrice over something that might
very well be nothing. She had no idea how Rothwell
would react, but she had a hunch that he would not
take such news well. She knew of only one person
she dared trust with the story of the strange man in
the stables, and that was Evan. He knew Rothwell
better than she, and he would no doubt know what
to do.

She did not hesitate a moment longer for fear that
she might change her mind altogether. She rushed
out of her room and down the hall to where she
knew Beatrice had placed Evan. She stood outside
his door, her heart racing. She raised her hand to
knock, only to let it drop. What would he think of
her?

Quelling her nervousness and taking a calming
deep breath, she knocked lightly on the door and
waited.

Evan opened his door. Surprise mixed with something close to fear registered upon his face when he
saw her. "Miranda."

"Please, just let me in," she said as she pushed her way past him into his bedchamber before she lost her nerve completely.

"What are you doing here?" He stood lithe and graceful in his shirtsleeves, black knee breeches, and white stockings. His cravat had been removed to reveal a strong column of bare throat. He looked wary.

"It might be nothing at all," she said.

"What is it?"

She started pacing. "I did not know whom I should tell."

"Tell what? Miranda, out with it." His voice sounded troubled indeed.

She sat down upon a settee in front of the fire that crackled and hissed in the grate and looked up at him as he stood next to the fireplace. "I was in the stables."

"When?"

"Just after I left you in the courtyard." She felt herself color slightly. "I could not bear to go back to the drawing room. I needed somewhere peaceful where I might go and think for a moment."

He leaned against the small desk and cocked an eyebrow. "Your chamber is not peaceful?"

"Of course it is, but I—oh, never mind, Evan." She felt flustered and not a little overwhelmed to be in his bedchamber. She glanced about in order to compose herself. His room was spacious and decorated in rich hues of gold and burnished rust.

His toiletries and sundries were meticulously arranged on his dressing table. His evening pumps were placed side by side on the floor in front of a chair, as if he had just removed them. "My goodness, how neat you are," she whispered, amazed. She had never thought him to be so tidy.

"Miranda," he sounded impatient. "What is it that you want? It is not at all the thing for you to be here."

"Of course not." Miranda forced herself to focus upon the reason she had come. "While I was in the stables, a man entered with neither a candle nor a lantern. In complete darkness he fumbled about, and when he tipped over a canister, he froze as if he did not wish to be discovered. I did not know what to think of it. I did not make my presence known, and so he did not realize that I watched him. It was too dark for me to see what he was up to."

Evan's expression was grave. "That does not sound good. Did you get a look at the man's face?"

"No. As I said, it was too dark. I was too far away, and he may have been wearing a cloak."

"Sinister indeed." Evan rubbed his jaw.

"Do you think so?"

Evan shrugged off his comment with a slight smile. "I shall have a talk with the groom at least, make him aware of the situation so that he can take precautions."

"Will you tell Rothwell?"

"Not yet. Keep your wits about you. Perhaps one of our guests is thinking of sabotage."

"Surely not," Miranda breathed. She could not imagine anyone planning something so foul.

"The Quorn does not always bring out the best in men," Evan said. "But then, perhaps I, too, am making too much of this."

Miranda nodded. She felt better with the weight of what she had seen off her shoulders and transferred to Evan's. Uncertain what else to say and feeling terribly conscious of the fact that she was in his bedchamber, Miranda cleared her throat. "Very well, I shall bid you good evening, then."

Evan stepped forward. He bowed low in order to offer her his arm, but she stood quickly. Their heads bumped with a resounding thud.

"Owww!" he cried. He backed away, rubbing his brow.

"Oh dear." She stepped toward him and reached out to touch his forehead with tentative fingers. "Evan, I beg your forgiveness, I did not realize."

"Sshhh. It is quite all right," his voice softened. "You have a knack for hurting me one way or another." His slanted smile threw her off guard.

She tried to ignore how close they were, but it was impossible. She could feel the warmth of him beckoning her to get yet closer. A stirring deep inside her made her feel weak. "Again, I beg your pardon," she said with a voice much deeper than normal. "— Forso many things," she added, with a whisper.

He said nothing. He only stared into her eyes.

She quickly looked away from the gray depths of his gaze. She noticed that as he leaned against the desk, his hands were braced along the side. His grip must indeed be tight, since his knuckles had turned completely white.

She concentrated upon feeling the top of his head. "There's a lump starting, I am afraid. Here, sit down." She ushered him to the settee and practically pushed him into it. Still he had not spoken to her, and she wondered if she had knocked him senseless.

She hastened to his washstand, poured cold water from the pitcher into the basin, and dipped in a cloth. After wringing it out, she returned to place the cold cloth upon his head. "There," she said softly. "Hold that for a moment or two." She backed away from him.

He obeyed. "Are *you* all right?"

"Of course I am," she answered. "I have a hard head."

He chuckled. "You always did." His eyes took on a far-off look, as if he remembered an incident from their past.

She wanted to know what he was thinking but was too much a coward to ask. They had so many memories. Some were sweet, and some were bitter indeed. She had forced herself not to dwell upon Evan after she had married Crandle. It had been sheer torture to remember the things they had done together, the ardent eagerness of his courtship.

And, now, she felt those memories flooding back as she looked at him. She had to say something to end the animosity between them. She stepped close and lifted the cloth to inspect the lump on his head. It did not appear to be getting any larger. It would no doubt be back to normal in a day or two. "Evan," she said, as she took the cloth from him and returned it to the water basin. "Might we call a truce of sorts?"

She felt him behind her. She could feel the goose-flesh upon her arms, and she chafed them with her hands. She turned around to look up into his eyes.

"Why did you marry him?" he asked gravely.

She sighed. She owed him the truth, the real explanation. In fact, it was long overdue. "My father had mortgaged Hemsley Manor to the hilt. He had sold off several parcels of land to our neighbor, Lord Crandle, for ready funds. Unfortunately, my father had no business sense. The land he sold was prime farmland that he needed to provide an income to the barony. With it gone, he only sank more deeply into debt."

She wondered why she had never told him this before. She might have saved them both from at least some of the bitterness. She had been a fool. "My Season came, and I took. My father had hopes of my making an advantageous match that would enable him to clear his obligations and eventually purchase back the land from Crandle."

"I was not well to grass then. In fact, I was little more than a pauper. Why did your father encourage my suit?" Evan asked.

"Because my father could not say no. Neither to me nor to my mother. He lavished us both with more than we could afford. I had no idea how things stood until one day I overheard my father talking with Lord Crandle in his study. My father had fallen behind in his payments, and Crandle demanded his due. My father said that he had spent all he had on my Season, and it was then that Crandle handed out the terms of a deal. If I married Lord Crandle, my father's debts would be forgiven, the lands would be returned, and Crandle would have no further claim upon him."

"I had no idea." Evan retreated back to the settee. He sat down heavily.

"No one did."

"And so your father agreed."

"No," Miranda said quietly. "My father refused. He told Crandle that I was already betrothed, that the announcement lay upon his desk, waiting to be delivered to the *Morning Post*."

She took a seat next to him on the settee. "Crandle did not take this news well. He rattled off the chain of events that would transpire as a result of my father defaulting on their contract. Crandle planned to take Hemsley. I was aghast. I could not stand by and let my brother's heritage and legacy die, all because I would follow my heart and marry you. I knew what had to be done. I ran into that room and agreed to Crandle's request. We were married not two days later by special license."

Evan ran a hand through his hair, feeling very low indeed. She had sacrificed her happiness and his to save her brother's future as heir. In her shoes, he wondered if he would not have done the same.

"So, you see, at the time I had no choice. But in hindsight, I wish I had sent you word of the real reason for my decision. But I was afraid to dishonor my father, and so I kept silent. For that I am truly sorry. Perhaps the outcome would have been different had I told you the truth."

Regret laced through him. "Or the very same—I had nothing."

He heard her sigh when she stood. She walked away from him and turned to lean against the desk. "So, that was my reason for marrying Crandle. I do wish we might put that behind us. Since we are here at Rothwell Park for such a short time, perhaps we might even cry friends."

He looked up into her eyes. He'd never considered a female a candidate for friendship before. Perhaps if they did become friends of sorts, the madness he felt in her presence would ease. He could not desire a friend, now, could he? It was worth a try.

"Very well," he said as he stood. "We shall endeavor to forge a friendship from this moment on." He extended his hand. Friends would shake on the matter. When he enveloped her soft palm into his own, he wondered why he had fussed so. They could be friends, and he'd finally find peace.

*   *   *

Early the next morning, Evan stood in Rothwell's study cooling his heels while Rothwell poured coffee for them both. By all that was holy, Evan's palms were damp. He did not quite know what made him more nervous, asking for Rothwell's permission to court his daughter or waiting for Rothwell's answer.

After the late night visit from Miranda, Evan decided that he must proclaim his intentions toward Artemis Rothwell. He refused to be thrown off his carefully considered plan by any misguided attraction for Miranda. He no longer loved her; he hardly knew her. What they had once felt for one another, the feelings they had shared, were a thing of the past. Evan did not care to examine his past any longer.

Nor did he wish to relive it.

He remained convinced that he must wed a young lady like Artemis Rothwell. They had many interests in common, and she would no doubt make him a comfortable wife. With her, he would continue his calm and calculated existence. His life would remain in order.

He had agreed to become friends with Miranda. He finally understood why she had jilted him all those years ago. The bitterness he had held against her softened. He felt cleansed from the pain he had endured, since it now appeared to be justified.

He felt renewed with that knowledge, and with that renewal came the clarity of mind he needed to offer for Artemis Rothwell.

"You wished to talk?" Rothwell asked with a satisfied gleam in his eye.

"Yes," Evan said, wondering why he felt completely tongue-tied.

"Well, spill it, man." Rothwell handed him a cup of steaming black coffee.

Evan took a sip and savored the taste of the strong brew. He looked over the rim of his cup at the man who might become his father-in-law. Rothwell was a man he respected, even admired, but he was not a patient man. Evan put his cup down and cleared his throat. "I wished to—" he hesitated. "I wanted to request permission to pay my addresses to your daughter." There, he had said it.

Rothwell leaned back in his chair, a lopsided grin on his face. "And about time too. I was hoping you'd get around to this last year. Of course you have my blessing to ask for my daughter's hand."

Evan relaxed. He had Rothwell's approval. "Last year, I was not quite ready to think about it."

"What has changed your mind?"

Evan realized that underneath the warm jovial exterior, Rothwell was indeed a shrewd man. He chose his words carefully. "I have reached an age where I must think about setting up my nursery. I am not getting any younger, and my estate is getting larger. I wish to leave it in good hands."

"I see. And you think my Artemis will make you happy?"

Evan had never truly given much thought to his happiness. For him, being content was enough. The pursuit of sheer happiness was next to foolishness. "I believe we shall suit, and I will be content. As to happiness, I do not believe anyone can tell until after the wedding."

Rothwell narrowed his eyes for only a moment, and then his face split into a wide grin and he laughed.

Evan smiled in return.

"I suppose you have the right of it." Rothwell rose from his chair. He was not a man to sit for very long. "I give you my full permission, but in the end, the decision is entirely Artemis'. She is very much a lady with her own mind. If it is you that she wants, so be it, and an announcement will be made." He reached out his hand.

Evan took it and shook hard. He felt relieved to have this over and done with, but he could not help but feel a tiny bit disappointed too. He brushed such nonsense aside; this was the reason he had come. He need only find Miss Rothwell and pose his offer to her.

After leaving Rothwell's study, it did not take Evan long to find the young lady he sought. Artemis Rothwell was where he would expect to find her. She stood in the stables, confidently overseeing the preparations for the upcoming hunt. Her father obviously trusted her judgment if he allowed her to order the grooms about regarding the stabling of each of the guests' horses. Prime horseflesh was not something to be trifled with or left to the ministrations of a novice. Evan experienced a swell of pride in the lady's knowledge and expertise. Yes, she was an admirable young woman. Now was the time to put forth his offer, before he lost his nerve.

"Good morning, Miss Rothwell," Evan said, as he stepped next to her.

"Lord Ashbourne, you rise early."

"I always have." He clasped his hands behind his back and took a deep breath. He did not wish to beat about the bush. He would come straight to the heart of the matter and get the thing done. "Miss Rothwell," he started.

She turned wide brown eyes upon him. "Yes?"

"I have spoken to your father this morning regarding . . ." He felt the words stick in his throat. He coughed to clear them. This was more difficult than he had anticipated. "You must understand, that although we have only just met, I find that I admire you, and I believe—" Again he stopped.

"Yes? You believe?" She looked eager, and that gave him encouragement.

"I believe that we might indeed suit comfortably. I have asked permission to pay my addresses to you, and your father has agreed. I humbly ask that you consider my suit. I would consider it a privilege should you agree to accept my offer of marriage."

There, he had done it. He had said what needed to be said, and if she accepted, then he'd be saved from any influences Miranda might have on him.

"Lord Ashbourne," Artemis said calmly. "You do me a great honor, and I assure you I will consider your offer with care. Please allow me to say that I must think on it."

Evan bowed. Again he admired the maturity with which she handled his offer. She did not dissolve into fits of giggles or any other such nonsense. "Of course," Evan said. "I shall look forward to your decision."

"Thank you. Now if you will excuse me, I must change into my riding habit." She tipped her head to the side as if considering a new idea. "I say, would you like to go for a ride? I can have Castlestone readied for you."

"A splendid idea. Shall I have Elias tacked with a sidesaddle for you?"

"Please do. I shall only be a moment."

Evan watched her depart. He had done what he came here to do, and it felt right. It made perfect sense. The trouble was that he kept seeing Miranda's disapproving gaze in his mind's eye.

The morning dawned bright. Sunlight streamed into the room when a maid drew back the curtains.

"What time is it?" Miranda asked with a raspy voice.

"Half past eight, Ma'am." The maid bobbed a curtsy and scurried to fill her basin with hot water. A pitcher of cold water stood nearby for her as well.

"Where is Babette?" Miranda wondered why her own maid had not come to wake her.

"She is bringing a tray to break your fast, my lady."

Miranda lay back. "I see." Curious. She wondered why Babette thought she would not wish to join the others in the breakfast room.

In moments, her maid entered with a tray laden with food.

"Bonjour, Madame. Ze did sleep well, non?"

"Oui," Miranda answered. She had, in fact, slept like the dead. Perhaps the strain of seeing Evan again, coupled with the excessive emotions she experienced last evening, had finally taken their toll.

She had a slight headache, which was only to be expected when one's feelings ran the gamut from extreme desire and frustration to downright fear when she was in the stables. But this morning was an entirely new day. And Evan had agreed to be her friend. It was indeed a start.

Miranda decided that she must at least make an attempt to recapture what she and Evan once shared. Love that deep did not happen twice in one's life. She doubted that she would ever feel that deeply for any other man.

She had received several proposals for discreet affairs from many gentlemen over the last seven years, but looking back every man paled in comparison to Evan.

She had often taken pride in the fact that she had honored her marriage vows, despite her unhappiness. The interesting twist was that she now wondered if she had simply measured every man against her memory of Evan. Those men had all come up sadly lacking, and Miranda had remained pure. But now she did not feel so pure. She felt heated with desire for Evan.

One person stood in the way of her pursuing Evan outright. That person was Artemis, and Miranda had no idea what could be done, since the man planned to offer for the girl.

Evan relished the warmth of the stables as he carefully inspected each horse stabled there while he waited for Miss Rothwell's return. Many of the male guests had brought at least two or three hunters with them. All told, there were upwards of fifty horses and each one appeared sound, but he would check them all more closely when time permitted.

He had spoken with one of the grooms while he saddled the horses. Rothwell's hunters were well known and well sold. The profits Rothwell realized from the sale of horseflesh after the Quorn were considerable. Rothwell was considered an expert. Some in the area believed that Rothwell deserved to be Master of the Quorn, instead of the nasty George Osbaldeston, who had earned the position last year.

Regardless, Evan knew that there was money at stake, and that tended to make some men desperate. He urged the groom to keep a close eye upon the stables since there were so many valuable hunters housed. Evan would inform Rothwell alone of what Miranda had seen if it proved necessary.

He had just finished tightening the girth on Castle-stone when Clasby sauntered into the stall, chewing on a long piece of hay.

"I say, Evan, you are up early. Trouble?"

"What makes you ask that? I've always been an early riser."

"I just left the breakfast room, and Lady Crandle was not present. I heard that she has the headache. Perhaps she did not have a good night's sleep, either from worry or other things . . ."

Evan tried to ignore the insinuation, but his friend's tone irked him. "What's your point?"

"My point is that I saw the fair lady enter your chamber last night."

Evan busied himself with adjusting the stirrups. He did not wish to discuss what had transpired with Clasby. Although he and Clasby had made sport of chasing some of the ladies present during the Quorn in the past, Evan did not want Miranda's name bandied about in such a manner. "It's not what you think."

A broad grin split Clasby's face as he leaned against the stall. "Care to share?"

"No."

"Oh, come now, do not say that you are becoming enamored of her all over again. What of your plans for Miss Rothwell?"

That brought Evan up short. He turned to Clasby. "You can be very annoying."

"Of course." He made a mock bow and waited.

Evan knew that unless he gave Clasby some information, the man would not let the matter drop. "We have made a truce," he explained as he led his horse out towards the open yard. "Lady Crandle and I shall become friends. I am not enamored of her."

Clasby snorted his contempt.

"What?" Evan asked.

"As if men and women could ever be friends."

Evan smiled. "Clasby, no matter how enlightened you pretend to be, you are primeval. It is the nineteenth century."

"Primeval, all knowing—they are interchangeable."

Evan shook his head. Clasby was one of the few men who truly held a high opinion of himself. He was not exactly conceited. He simply thought well of who he was. Evan actually envied him that comfort in himself. He had been striving to reach such a place. "My plans for Miss Rothwell remained unchanged. In fact I have just now offered for her." Evan nearly winced at the lack of conviction in his voice.

"Here in the stables?"

"Why not?" He was relieved that Clasby did not notice any waver in Evan's resolve.

"Not exactly the most romantic place."

"Perhaps not, but Miss Rothwell is level headed. We are in fact going to ride out together."

"Where are you headed?" Clasby asked.

"I'd like to meet with Rothwell's terrierman, see the new pups, get a good look at Rothwell's land. Care to join us?"

"I will not impose?"

"Of course not. It might make things a bit more comfortable. She has not yet accepted."

"It will take me only a moment to ready my horse."

Evan nodded. As he stood gazing across the Rothwell pastures and farmland, he realized that he'd be spending considerable time here. Artemis would no doubt wish to visit her family often. It was not an unpleasant prospect, but something about the reality of it hit him between the eyes. A seed of worry wiggled its way into his heart. What if he did not find contentment with his choice; what then?

He mentally shook off such petty doubts. He wished to inspect the vast property without the persuasive pride of Rothwell shining through every comment. He knew the marriage settlements that would come with Artemis Rothwell would be large, but he felt it was his duty to see proof of their worth for himself.

The subject of his thoughts materialized before his eyes. Artemis Rothwell, dressed in a dark violet riding habit, walked towards him. He realized that he had spent far too little time alone with her since he had arrived. It was time to correct that, even if Clasby was along as makeshift chaperone.

"I say, Miss Rothwell, you look smashing this morning. I hope you do not mind that Ashbourne has invited me along," Clasby said.

Her smile was ready, and Evan assured himself again that she would do well by him. "Of course not." She turned a saucy grin toward Evan. "Where to?" she asked boldly.

"Your father's terrierman."

"Wonderful," she answered. "Now, Lord Ashbourne, I promised to show you my father's prized hunter's mettle. Castlestone will give the Quorn a fine go. And he'll give you a ride you won't forget."

"Very well. Elias is tacked for you, although he's not too happy about the sidesaddle. He will obey your every command."

"Then let us hurry Mr. Clasby along and be off," Artemis said.

Miranda watched from a hall window that over-looked the stable yard where Mr. Clasby, Evan, and Artemis mounted their horses. She noticed that Artemis rode Evan's hunter, and her heart experienced a pang of something she was not quite ready to identify as jealousy. The two did have much in common, and yet she wondered if love would ever be one of them. Artemis beamed under his attention as any young woman would.

Miranda shook her head and stepped away from the window, her hopes dashed considerably. She could not falter in her resolve to see Artemis suitably wed to a man who loved her, yet what if she fell in love with Evan?

At least tomorrow evening Artemis would have the chance to practice her dancing skills at the local assembly's All Hallow's Eve Ball. Perhaps there she might meet a young gentleman who could turn her head.

The house was still quiet as she made her way back to her chamber. The ladies were no doubt still abed, as were Beatrice and Rothwell. And she planned to return to her bed herself for a much needed nap.

Her head pounded in earnest. Too many thoughts of Evan. She was determined to be his friend, but she knew mere friendship would never satisfy her. She felt a restlessness she had not experienced when they were at odds. She could not shake the feeling of expectancy, of wanting to see him.

She had to keep herself in control of her senses where Evan was concerned. Friendship was good. It was a beginning that could prove to be the healing balm they needed after their bitterness. If she was careful, she might nurture that friendship into warmer feelings. But she must indeed tread carefully. Evan had made it very clear that he wanted nothing more than friendship from her.

Chapter Eight

*L*ater that morning, Miranda heard a commotion in the main hall, and she hurried her steps. Descending the stairs, she took in the scene before her. Evan, Mr. Clasby, and Artemis had returned from their ride, and they stood with Rothwell and Beatrice. Evan looked unsettled but calm. Mr. Clasby remained the quiet observer as Artemis rapidly explained what had happened to her father.

"Castlestone took ill." Artemis gestured broadly, her voice shrill. She was indeed upset. "He acts like he is winded, even though he should not be. We walked a good portion of the way home."

By now, several of the guests had wandered into the enormous entrance hall, wondering what was amiss. They looked on with curious stares as Rothwell hurried out of the door, calling over his shoulder not to hold luncheon for him.

"Castlestone is our best hunter," Artemis said to no one in particular. "He might fetch upwards of three hundred pounds, but not as he is now. He looks positively horrible."

At that moment, Evan looked up to where Miranda stood motionless upon the stairs. She cocked a questioning eyebrow. *Could this have something to do with the man she had spied in the stables?* she wondered, as she made her way down to join the group.

"I know, dear. Your father will take care of it." Beatrice wrapped her arm around her daughter's shoulders with a comforting squeeze. "Come, luncheon will be served shortly. You will want to clean up."

Miranda stepped close to Evan and whispered, "What should we do?"

"Nothing just yet," he said. "But keep your eyes and ears open."

Evan entered the dining room, his gaze sweeping every guest for signs of unease or traces of guilt. He could discern neither. He leaned close to Miranda, who walked in front of him. The clean scent of her hair enticed him to inhale again. He wondered if she had just washed it.

The sunlight streaming through the windows reflected glimmers of gold in the long tresses she wore wrapped neatly about her head. He remembered exactly how her hair had looked that night when she had broken the glass. It was loosed in all its auburn glory, and even then, he wanted to bury his hands and face in it.

The Deuce! He pulled his wayward thoughts firmly back to the business at hand. He leaned closer to Miranda's ear. "Does anyone look to you as if they could have been the man in the stables?" he whispered.

She turned to look at him, and he felt his body react. She smelled too good, and her smooth skin dared him to reach out and touch her. He firmly clasped his hands behind his back to keep himself from acting on the impulse. This was completely ridiculous. He had no business thinking of Miranda this way. They had cried friends. And he had asked Rothwell's daughter to marry him.

"I did not see the man's face," she said quietly.

"Compare statures, then." Evan moved away from her before they drew the attention of the others. If the man in the stable was a guest, he did not wish to alarm him. Even so, he needed her help to point him out. Evan watched as Miranda scrutinized each male in the room. She looked them over carefully, weighing each man's height and breadth of shoulders against those of the man she had seen in the stables.

He had to own it was not easy for him to watch her stare so keenly at other gentlemen. He felt the heat rise around the collar of his shirt, and he wanted to pull at his cravat, as if it had suddenly become too tight. He forced himself to relax when she looked up at him and shook her head. None of them appeared to match the man she had seen in the stables.

Luncheon was an informal affair with no assigned seating. Evan chose to sit next to Artemis in order to question her. He could not tell her the situation he suspected until he knew more. It might simply be a coincidence that Castlestone had become ill the day after Miranda saw the man in the stable. Even so, he needed to find out all he could.

He poured lemonade for both Artemis and himself. He looked up to catch Miranda's gaze upon him. She sat next to Clasby, who chattered gaily at her side, but she appeared not to hear a word. A slight frown marred her brow. He gave her a nod of encouragement. She did not appear to be her usual composed self today, and he wondered why.

But then the thought that perhaps one of Rothwell's guests was tampering with the horses put one's back up. He could not blame her for appearing slightly rattled. He turned his attention to Artemis. "What did you think of Elias?"

"He is fine, indeed. Sired from the same bloodline as Castlestone, but of course you must know that. I only wish that Castlestone had not been ill. He is a superior ride even to your mount," Artemis said.

"Your father often sells his hunters this time of year, does he not?"

"Of course. After the Quorn, he has many buyers. My father has only to ride them, or have a trusted friend ride them, and many gentlemen fall over themselves to purchase them, outbidding each other in turn."

"I see."

"Aye," Lord Cole, seated to their far right, added. "Rothwell's reputation for the finest horseflesh in the Midlands is well known."

At that moment, Rothwell entered the dining room to join them. He looked harried but also relieved.

"How is he, Papa?" Artemis asked.

"He'll be fine in a few days. Colic. Don't know what he could have eaten to bind him up so." Rothwell sat down next to his wife, who patted his hand. "Our groom has an excellent remedy. We shall have to wait it out over the next couple of days. Even so, we have to keep Castlestone on his feet. A couple of the boys are taking turns walking him about."

"Come now, dear, let us speak of more pleasant things," Lady Rothwell said.

"Did you hear that there is a grand fair in Shepeshed?" Mr. Clasby asked.

"A fair?" The Waterton-Symthe sisters asked in tandem. "We should love to go."

"I do not know," Lady Rothwell wavered. She

looked to Miranda for help, who shrugged her shoulders.

Several guests rallied to point out that a fair in honor of the Quorn was something not to be missed. Artemis fairly begged to go, and when her mother continued to hesitate in granting her approval, Evan intervened. Such an outing would give him a chance to ask some discreet questions of the locals without raising any concern. Rothwell had a reputation for selling prime horseflesh at higher than top dollar. He'd bet a monkey someone did not wish that to happen this year.

After luncheon, Miranda changed into a warm carriage dress of Mexican blue kerseymere with ivory lace accenting the bodice and cuffs. As she stared at herself in the looking glass, she had to own that she was indeed satisfied with this new steel blue color. She thought it complemented her hazel eyes very well as it brought out more of the gold.

An unbidden vision of Evan's eyes swirled in her mind. His eyes were the color of a cloudy day. She used to read his mood in them long ago. Now they had become shuttered, as if he gathered clouds of his own to block out the light from his soul.

She donned a pair of dark gray half boots of kid leather, pushing her fanciful thoughts aside as she pulled on a fur-lined pelisse. The day had turned cool, and she was glad for the added warmth. Their outing to the fair in the neighboring town of Shepeshed would be an all-day event.

A quick knock at the door brought her head up as Artemis stepped into her chamber. "Are you ready?" she asked.

"I am. Come, let me look at you." Miranda motioned for her to step closer. "Artemis, that dress is lovely on you."

Artemis made a face. "Too frilly, I think." The rust color warmed the girl's flawless ivory skin, making her dusky hair shine with soft lights of brown and red. Tiny slashes in the long sleeves and hem had deep gold silk pulled through into little puffs. Artemis resembled a grand lady of the manor.

"Your mother has chosen your wardrobe well," Miranda said.

"With thoughts only of catching a husband. I cannot ride in such a gown, and I feel compelled to keep it clean since it cost a near fortune."

Miranda laughed, and then said, "Artemis, you are too practical by far. Have none of the gentlemen caught your fancy, then?"

"I am happy with things as they are." Artemis looked away as she spoke, and Miranda wondered if perhaps she did not quite speak the truth.

"You are a grown lady now. Do you not wish for a home of your own?"

"I have a home," Artemis said, with a mulish tilt to her chin.

Miranda let the matter drop. She thought that if she continued on the subject, Artemis would stubbornly continue to be vague about her desires for the future. "Tell me about this fair," Miranda said instead.

"It is a ripping event. I am glad that Ashbourne talked Mama into going. She thinks the Quorn Fair a coarse display of country ignorance and inappropriate behavior, but I quite love it. We went last year."

"Yes, indeed." Miranda had not been to a country fair since before her come-out. The fairs near her childhood home of Hemsley were merely quaint gatherings. Shepeshed was bound to be crowded with rowdy young bucks and gentlemen of wealth and position. And therein lay the allure. Society condescended to rub elbows with the common folk when it meant an evening of unrestrained entertainment.

"How was your ride this morning?" Miranda asked, as she pulled on her gloves. She wondered where they had gone.

"Perfection, until Castlestone took sick. We visited the terrierman to see the new puppies. I should love one of them, but Father says they will fight with his hounds. Ashbourne said a terrier is not a good pet. He hates them, calls them little nippers."

"Truly?" Miranda did not like the fact that she yearned for more details of their conversation. She wanted to know every word that Evan had said, and she feared it might show. For the first time, she felt awkward in Artemis' presence.

She wondered again if Artemis had become attracted to Evan. It was obvious that she admired him, but was she forming a real *tendre* for him? The thought did not sit well with Miranda. She wanted the best for Artemis, a love match that would make her happy the rest of her days.

But not with Evan.

Miranda wanted Evan for herself, but she did not wish to pay the price of Artemis' heartache in the process. Worry stirred in the depths of her heart. And then there was Beatrice—how could she possibly hurt her dearest friend's daughter? It was not to be borne, and yet, Miranda knew Evan was not right for Artemis.

"Miranda, what is it?" Artemis touched her arm.

"I beg your pardon."

"You were miles away just now. Is anything wrong?"

Miranda shook her head and smiled. "Nothing in the least. I was simply woolgathering. Come, let us go downstairs and join the others. We do not wish to keep them waiting."

The entire party left for the fair. The ladies climbed into several carriages, while the men accompanied them on horseback. Spirits were high with anticipation. Miranda rode with Beatrice, Artemis, and Miss Whitlow. The picturesque countryside dotted with flocks of grazing sheep gave way to winding roads that led into the village of Shepeshed not more than ten miles east of Rothwell Park.

The village was much larger than Miranda had expected. The clack of hooves echoed through the near empty cobbled streets, as they wound their way through the town crowded with homes and cottages nestled against each other. Rambling wild rosebushes sported bright red rose hips along the lanes.

Beatrice explained that Shepeshed was an important market in the wool trade. Most of the inhabitants worked with knitting frames. And most were at the fair on the far outskirts of town. "I buy all my woolens here," Beatrice said.

"A lovely town," Miranda added.

"With a large turnout of the local gentry and landowners for the All Hallow's Eve Ball," Beatrice said. "Tomorrow evening we shall make this journey again, only it will be to the assembly rooms."

Miranda nodded. The ball would give Artemis a fine chance to use her newly acquired dancing skills. She hoped that romance would indeed be in the air

that night. She looked forward to a dance or two
with Evan.

They drove through Shepeshed until they reached
an expanse of open fields. They pulled into an area
filled with a bazaar of booths and stalls. Merchants
and farmers alike sold their wares, baked goods, and
cheeses. Several horse traders haggled with gentlemen interested in purchasing an extra mount for
the Quorn.

Merriment and laughter filled the air. Music
floated on the chilly breeze, as did incredible smells
of sweet breads and cinnamon. Miranda found herself smiling; she felt young again. Several of the ladies darted off in small groups, Artemis being swept
into one of them by Miss Whitlow. She noted that
Evan followed a group of the men to a stall filled
with pistols and muskets.

Rothwell looked ready to purchase a matched set
of pistols, when Beatrice noticed. "Come," she said
as she looped her arm through Miranda's. "I must
stop him from buying something he does not need."

Miranda laughed and followed where Beatrice led.
Beatrice managed Rothwell in many ways, but the
love they had for one another shimmered through
clear and true. When they reached the stall, she
turned to see Evan testing the weight of a pistol. A
chill raced down her spine as she watched him gently
raise and aim the weapon to test it.

"Are you going to purchase that?" She stood next
to him.

"I may. I did not bring one of my own." He kept
closing one eye and squinting as he raised the gun
to a mock target.

Memories of Evan involved in duels flooded into
her brain, chilling her completely. During her Season,

Evan had participated in three duels. He had seconded a friend once, and he had fought two of his own. Once, he had challenged a man who had acted inappropriately toward her at a ball. The two had met at dawn, but fortunately, the other man shot off, ending the match without bloodshed.

At the time, she had been so young and stupid that she had thought the whole thing rather gallant. Now she knew better, and the sight of Evan holding a weapon with such cool resolve bothered her.

"Evan," she whispered. "You frighten me. Surely there is no need to go to such lengths. I may have made something out of nothing when I saw that man in the stable." She laid her hand upon his arm. "There is no need for this."

"It is good to be prepared," he said through tight lips.

Miranda bit her tongue. She'd not argue with him. She looked at Rothwell and Beatrice, who urged her husband not to purchase the pair of pistols. Rothwell finally gave in and put them back, and the two moved on to the next booth hand in hand.

Evan saw the exchange as well. He looked as though he had just eaten something that did not agree with him.

"He did not need them," Miranda said quietly. "I have seen his collection of guns and muskets. I assure you it is vast."

"Does it matter?" He put down the pistol he held and looked at her. "Rothwell should purchase what he chooses, when he wishes."

"What of Beatrice?" Miranda felt her defenses rise. "May she purchase with the same freedom?"

He looked at her as if she had grown a second head. "Of course not!"

"And why not?"

"Because Rothwell holds the purse strings, or at least he should."

"Evan," Miranda said, as if she spoke to a simpleton. "What makes you think Rothwell is adept at such a task?"

When he had no answer, she continued with her point. "Look at my father. He nearly lost everything because my mother never bothered to inquire about the purse strings."

Evan looked ready to argue, but instead, he shook his head. "That was different." He returned the pistol to its case, much to the merchant's disappointment. Two sales had just been lost.

Miranda felt relieved. She did not wish Evan to come to violence over Rothwell's horses. The true art of being a gentleman was the ability to settle disagreements in an honorable fashion without bloodshed.

She looked about, but she did not see a single guest from the Rothwell house party. "What shall we do now?" She was alone with Evan, and she was glad. They needed to nourish the friendship they had agreed to, and that required time in each other's company.

He offered her his arm without hesitation, but she saw the wariness in his eyes. Disappointment gnawed at her heart. She supposed that she could not expect him to want to be in her presence, even though they had agreed to a truce. She was surprised at how much it hurt to know that he wished to be gone from her. Even so, he escorted her about the booths until they had seen most of the merchants' wares.

"What else interests you?" he asked politely.

"I should very much like to find out what is going on over there." She pointed at the crowd gathered near a large tent.

"Then let us proceed."

They walked in silence, and Miranda's thoughts rolled in turmoil. She had the ability to spare herself much grief as long as she kept her wits and used her head where Evan was concerned. She could hardly throw herself at him, nor did she wish to be rejected by him outright.

She bit her lower lip. Part of her had died when she married Crandle. Spending time with Evan was bringing back to life what she thought she had lost. She would not allow herself a repeat partial death by having her heart broken, and yet she craved more of the life Evan had breathed into her.

Evan pulled Miranda close as they bumped their way through the throng of people. Her reaction to his nearness was immediate and intense. She felt the warmth of his body seep into her even through her thick pelisse. Every nerve ending in her fingers tingled. She itched to touch him, and yet she did not dare. She peeked up at him. Might he feel the same draw?

Cheers from the crowd went up, capturing her attention. Pound notes were passed back and forth amidst a gathering of men from all walks of life. Lofty gentlemen and farmers both made wagers on something.

She and Evan inched their way forward into a slight break in the wall of people until they saw what caused the commotion. Artemis was engaged in an archery match with Mr. Clasby. By all accounts, it looked as if Artemis was winning.

Miranda jerked forward as if intending to stop this

display, but Evan held her back. "Wait a moment. You will only cause a scene if you charge over there and yank her away," he said quietly.

"But what of her reputation? It is hard enough to battle her appearance as a romp."

"Rothwell will laugh at the situation, proud his daughter could beat out a renowned rake at archery. As for Lady Rothwell, you know her better than I."

"I cannot think she will be pleased. Only look at the expression on the Waterton-Smythe sisters."

Evan glanced their way and chuckled. "They are merely jealous." The entire scene did not bother him a whit. He needed no London miss with a sterling reputation for flattery and flutters. Having a wife who was renowned as a fine archer gave him no pause. In fact, it amused him.

Miranda was not satisfied. "Perhaps, but even so, Artemis should not be known as a hoyden. It is not the thing, I assure you."

He let out a sigh. "Well then, let us intervene."

"How?"

"By becoming their partners." Evan pulled her along into the clearing where Artemis and Clasby stood poised with bow and arrows. "Mind if we join you?"

Clasby turned with a bright smile of welcome and nodded. Artemis looked almost irritated at the interruption when she saw Miranda. "I am about to beat Mr. Clasby thoroughly," she said.

"Yes, but you may cause your mother distress by your athletic display," Evan whispered for Artemis' ears alone. He bent down to pick up a large bow and tested it.

Artemis colored slightly but held her head high, a

look of defiance in her eyes. "Very well." She gave over to the disappointed sighs of the crowd.

Evan gathered up arrows. "Shall we continue as a team?"

"By all means." Artemis waved to the men at the straw target, who then removed the arrows for a new match. "Ladies against men?" she asked with an impish smile.

"I think not," he answered. "You and I shall challenge Clasby and Lady Crandle." He turned to Clasby, who had his arms draped about Miranda in an attempt to show her how to use the bow.

He saw red.

He stepped forward, his heart pumping hard in his chest and his head ringing with sheer jealous rage. He was ready to charge in and knock Clasby on his ear when he caught himself. Taking a deep breath, he calmed his irrational surge of temper. He hated the unmanageable feelings that washed over him when it came to Miranda. He swore she was the only woman on earth who evoked such madness in him.

"Excuse me," he said to Artemis. He heard his own calm voice, but it was as if another man spoke. "I believe we have the advantage as we are. I shall join Lady Crandle and send Clasby to you."

Artemis looked at him sharply, not at all pleased with his suggestion, but she said nothing. She picked up her bow and arrows, looking very much the image of her Roman counterpart, Diana the Huntress.

"Clasby," Evan called, "let us switch places. I fear we shall trounce you and Lady Crandle as we are."

Clasby smiled. It was a broad, all-knowing grin that irked Evan all the more. He had lost his ability to reason when he saw Miranda in the arms of another. By all that was holy, Clasby knew that.

"I warn you," Miranda said, "I am no good at sporting activities and especially bad at archery."

A sudden vision of them engaged in an activity requiring close contact flitted through his mind. He gritted his teeth, trying to wipe out the image of Miranda lying in his arms. "I am a much better archer than Clasby," he explained. "You two would not have had a chance."

"I am your disadvantage then."

He ignored the urge to tell her that she had always been his disadvantage. "Have you ever pulled a bow before?" he asked instead.

"Once, during my Season," she said softly.

Evan came to stand behind her. "Then let me help you. Position the arrow, and bring up your bow." He placed his arms about her in order to show her how to maintain the height of her elbow. "Hold it steady, like so." He let his hand curl around the bend of her arm. "Keeping your arm firm, pull back the string between your two fingers and thumb. Keep your eye upon the tip of the arrow in aim of your target, and then release it."

Evan watched the arrow veer to the far right of the target, missing it completely as it flew into the woods.

Familiarity plagued him until he realized that they had done this before. It was *he* who had shown her how to use a bow during her Season. He had nibbled playfully at her neck when he stood behind her, whispering his devotion into her ear in order to throw off her aim.

Shaken by the memory, he looked down at her

beautifully formed nape. He stepped back from her. "There, I think you have it," he said.

"Are you ready?" Clasby asked.

"We are. Miss Rothwell may go first." Evan stood by and watched as Artemis took up her bow with perfect form. Her stance was firm and her arm steady as she launched her arrow with accuracy into the middle ring of the target. She stood proud and cast him a pert look of challenge to do better.

He glanced at Miranda when he picked up his own bow. The two ladies could not be more different. Where Artemis was bold, Miranda was reserved. Where Artemis was hard and defiant, Miranda was soft and pleading.

He took a deep steadying breath. Marrying Artemis would be the best thing for him. He knew in the depths of his soul that she would not keep him from leading his own life and properly managing his own estates. She would not demand that he dance attendance upon her or take her to London every spring.

He doubted, however, that Artemis Rothwell would ever cause his temperature to rise in a matter of seconds simply by looking at him. She would not wreak havoc with his senses or his better judgement. He'd not be tempted to give up everything he had become just to taste her lips or feel her body against his own. Of this he was quite certain.

Miranda would lead him to an early grave from the vast swings of emotions he experienced in her presence. He refused to become a jealous beast that would trample his best friend because he dared touch her. He ran a shaky hand through his hair before positioning his bow.

His decision was made, and he was glad of it. He had only the remainder of the week to resist the temptation that was Miranda. When he had pulled her close because of the crowd, he had read the desire in her eyes. She wanted him, it was plain to see. But he would not allow himself to get caught in her web of desire.

He let his arrow fly, and it landed true in the middle of the target, splitting Artemis' arrow in two.

Chapter Nine

*M*iranda pulled back upon the bow's string exactly as Evan had shown her. Her fingers shook slightly, and her spine still tingled from being in his arms, even if only for a lesson in archery. He had remembered the last time he had instructed her thus. Miranda knew the memory had sobered him, because he had suddenly backed away from her.

She let go of the string with a thump, and her arrow flew to the target. It hit the outer ring. She earned no points, but at least the arrow did not veer off and disappear into the woods, making her look like a fool.

She turned to Evan and smiled. She was improving in her aim, but still they were losing to Artemis and Mr. Clasby. He nodded in return, before taking up his bow. He was completely serious. He did not wish to lose. Even his dimples seemed to have flattened and disappeared, as if afraid to show themselves.

Miranda watched him move, taking pleasure in the mere sight of him. His shoulders were broader than when they had first met. In fact, Evan had grown more handsome with age. The fine lines etched in the corners of his eyes told the tale of a seasoned man, but when he smiled, his dimples gave way to an almost boyish charm that was devastating.

Artemis took up her bow again after Mr. Clasby scored with an arrow in the second ring of the target. Artemis demonstrated more than a simple desire to win. She was out to prove herself superior. Miranda could not help but wonder if Artemis' slight change in attitude had something to do with her.

There was an undeniable edge to her glance, and Miranda felt a pang of guilt. No doubt her attraction for Evan was showing through. What Miranda felt for Evan had grown into a tangible thing she feared she could no longer control. But control it she must, until she was sure of what Evan wanted. If Evan refused her affection, there would be no point in entertaining her hopes and desires for him. Perhaps she should let him come to her. She immediately dismissed that thought. He would never come, if left to his own devices.

Frustration burned in her belly. *Why did he not want her?*

It was her turn. She wearied of this game and cared even less for the outcome. She took up her bow and pulled its string with all her might, letting the arrow fly without bothering to aim. Her arrow soared through the crisp evening air and landed in the center ring. She had scored three points, closing the lead.

"Good show," Mr. Clasby called.

"Indeed," Evan added. "What did you do to make your aim so true?"

Miranda felt her cheeks color. "I do not recall," she said. How could she possibly confess to being frustrated by her longing for him?

"Sheer luck," Artemis said in an attempt at humor. The hard glint in her eyes told Miranda that Artemis was not pleased with her. "I will wager that you cannot repeat your score."

The crowd cheered, ready for yet another round of wagers.

"Artemis," Miranda said, with a light scold, "I did not believe you cared only to win. This is supposed to be in fun."

"In some things, winning is a must."

Miranda did not think they were speaking of archery. She glanced at Evan, who looked a bit uncomfortable with their exchange. He said nothing but took up his bow with a deep frown.

The crowd had grown even larger. Pound notes exchanged hands, and murmurs settled into silence in anticipation of Evan's turn at the bow. Miranda recognized Rothwell in the crowd. He looked on with pleasure, but beside him stood Beatrice looking concerned.

Miranda felt horrible and beset with guilt. She had been asked to Rothwell Park to help ease Artemis' way amongst society misses and the young men who'd make proper husbands. Now she found herself in competition for the same man's attention. But Evan was not right for Artemis! Somehow, she had to prove that to them both.

When it was her turn, Miranda squared her shoulders. She was not about to shrink from Artemis' challenge. She would indeed do her best to repeat her performance. She took great care to aim for the center of the target before she let go of her arrow. It hit the third ring with a disappointing thud. Her meager one point was not enough to take the lead. In the end, Artemis and Mr. Clasby trounced them soundly.

The crowd cheered, and Artemis was hailed by

many of the young bucks as a true-to-life goddess.
She was Diana reborn. Miranda overheard many ask
Artemis if she planned to attend the All Hallow's
Eve Ball the following evening.

The Waterton-Smythe sisters were green with envy
as they pushed their way into the circle of admirers
surrounding Artemis. Artemis handled the situation
well, agreeing to save a dance for each young man
who asked her. Artemis also pushed Miss Whitlow
forward, and despite her bruised feelings, Miranda's
heart swelled with pride. At least Artemis had remained agreeable toward those she counted as
friends.

When Evan held out his arm, Miranda took it with
ease. "Ashbourne, you have competition," she said
with a smile.

"That I do," he agreed, looking slightly worried.

"They are more suited to her age," Miranda reminded him.

"So you have said before."

Dinner was served late and without fanfare since
many had eaten treats at the fair. The gentlemen lingered long over their port, no doubt making plans
for the Quorn. Many of the ladies retired early, and
Miranda was one of them. The day spent out of
doors in the cold had exhausted her.

Artemis had kept a distinctly cool distance, which
bothered Miranda more than she cared to admit. She
had never wished for them to be at odds. After the
archery competition, Miranda and Evan had parted
ways. He had wished to talk with the locals about
whose horseflesh was up for sale this year. He hoped
to gain information where he could, in an attempt to
know more about the man in the stables.

Miranda had spent the rest of the time at the fair with Beatrice and Rothwell. Neither one had been greatly bothered by the archery match, much to Miranda's relief. Beatrice was grateful that Evan and Miranda had intervened to make the whole thing more acceptable. Although Beatrice encouraged Artemis to excel at all that she tried, she did not wish her daughter to be ridiculed or condemned as a hoyden.

It was nearly midnight when Miranda woke, with no hope of falling back to sleep. She read but to no avail. What she needed was a soothing cup of chamomile tea. Rousing out of bed, she drew on her nightrobe and headed for the kitchens.

Careful not to wake anyone, Miranda padded quietly through the hall. She descended the stairs and was making her way to the kitchens when she heard soft voices. Passing the small family drawing room, Miranda was surprised to hear feminine laughter. She peeked her head inside.

"Lady Crandle," Miss Whitlow said with surprise. "I hope we did not wake you."

"Of course not." She entered. Not a single candle burned. Only the light of a brightly burning fire that had been stoked with large logs illuminated the room. Several young ladies sat upon the floor in a half circle, a pail of hazelnuts in the center. "What are you doing?"

"We are finding out who our future husbands will be," Miss Whitlow explained.

The rest of the girls looked anxious, as if she might chase them all to bed and cast their game aside as pure foolishness.

"Would you care to join us?" Artemis asked.

Miranda hesitated. There was no warmth in the

smile Artemis gave her. Her eyes held a hint of challenge.

"Please do," Miss Whitlow exclaimed sweetly. "It will be such fun."

"Very well." Miranda took a seat upon the floor where they had made room. She sat next to Artemis, who handed her four hazelnuts. "What do I do?"

"Carve the letter of a gentleman's name into the shell," Artemis explained as she handed Miranda a knife. "Then, place them upon the fire screen. The one that pops back to you will be the man you will marry."

"I see." Most of the ladies had several hazelnuts. "What if I cannot think of four gentlemen?"

"Then scratch them all with the same letter, if there is only one man," Miss Whitlow said with a giggle.

Miranda felt her heart skip a beat when she thought of Evan. It was a childish game and yet she could not deny the thrill of it. And she felt young, incredibly young, as she sat cross-legged with ladies nearly eight years her junior.

She could hardly carve all the hazelnuts with an *E*, so she recklessly included Mr. Clasby and another young lord in the mix. When she was done with her carving, Miranda watched as each girl took her turn.

The girls chanted over and over, "If you love me/ Pop and fly/ If you hate me/ burn and die."

Miranda was caught up in the fervor as well, and she chanted along with them. Several girls lost all their hazelnuts to the fire, but a couple of the ladies retrieved a hot hazelnut with delight and pleasure in their husbands foretold.

Finally, it was Miranda's turn. They chanted until the heat caused two of the nuts to crackle and pop. Both fell into the flames. They chanted again. The last two hazelnuts wiggled, then quite literally flew from the screen into their circle. The ladies squealed and rolled out of the way of the hot flying hazelnuts.

"Two!" Miss Whitlow said, still laughing. "You are fortunate indeed. Perhaps you will have to choose which husband to take."

Miranda drew the hazelnuts toward her. They were still too warm to hold, so she turned them over quickly with the blade of Artemis' knife. The letter *E* was scratched on both.

"The same letter, the same man," Artemis said blandly. "It must indeed come true. Who is it, I wonder—my lord *E*?"

"No!" Miss Whitlow cried. "You cannot tell, or it will not come true. Artemis, it is your turn."

Miranda could not discern Artemis' mood. When they had chanted until the hazelnuts popped and fell, Artemis was left with only one that rolled upon the floor, steam rising from it. Artemis used her knife to flip it over. Miranda saw the carved *A*.

Ashbourne!

Miranda looked into Artemis' eyes and read the challenge there. Suddenly uncomfortable, Miranda stood. "Ladies, I must bid you good evening. I thank you for including me. I did indeed enjoy the game."

"But you mustn't leave yet," one of the ladies complained.

"Thank you, but I was headed for the kitchens to fetch a cup of chamomile tea. I shall complete my errand and then turn in for the night."

"I will help you," Artemis said.

Miranda felt her heart drop to her feet. Artemis wanted to either talk or pull caps, and Miranda dreaded them both. "Thank you."

The two of them walked silently to the kitchens

until Miranda could stand it no more. Once inside the vaulted ceilings of the Rothwell kitchen, Miranda turned to Artemis. "Please tell me what is on your mind that you glare at me so."

Artemis rolled her eyes but tossed back her hair that had been left undone. "What the does the *E* stand for? I know it must be Ashbourne."

Miranda dodged the question. "What makes you think so?"

"You have constantly been in his company, practically hanging upon him, in fact. I think it disgraceful."

Miranda reached out to touch Artemis' hand, but Artemis pulled hers back. It nearly broke Miranda's heart. "Artemis, that is unfair."

"You are trying to take him from me, I know that you are. Ashbourne is intended for me."

Miranda put aside her hurt and ignored Artemis' acid tone. "Do you truly wish to marry Lord Ashbourne? Think on it—you hardly know him."

"What of you? You met him only three days ago."

"That is not quite true. I knew Lord Ashbourne during my Season many years ago."

Artemis digested this information as she ran her finger along the top of the rough-hewn maple table. "Was he a suitor?"

"Yes." Miranda was not about to explain their history in depth. When Artemis did not answer, Miranda pushed forward. "Do you care for him, truly?"

"Perhaps." Artemis looked away.

At her uncertainty, Miranda softened. She reached out and stroked Artemis' cheek. "Be certain, be absolutely certain of your heart before you agree to spend your life with such a man."

Artemis' eyes widened. "What do you mean?"

"Evan—that is his Christian name—" Miranda explained, "wants his life to remain neat and orderly. Love is not like that. Love is inconvenient and tumultuous. I do not wish you to be placed into one of his tidy little categories for the sole purpose of begetting heirs. He has his estate and title, his outdoor pursuits, and his horses."

"You do not think he can love me?" Artemis asked.

"Of course he can. But do you not wish to be certain of his love before you give yourself in marriage? Why, only days ago you swore to remain unwed. What has altered your opinion?"

Again, Artemis traced the carved grooves of the table. "He is considered a prime catch," she said. Again, she seemed to be hiding something.

It dawned on Miranda that perhaps Ashbourne's sudden appeal was the fact that he was indeed a prize to be won. "He is, but there are others just as prime."

"Not here," Artemis said reluctantly.

"Perhaps not here, but in London, most certainly. I could take you there." Miranda held her breath.

Artemis looked up. "What would I do there?"

"There are so many things to do. There are museums and shops. The theater and the Egyptian Hall in Piccadilly. And there is Astley's Royal Amphitheater. Artemis, you would love that; it is a showcase of equestrian spectacles and shows." Miranda knew she had chipped a dent in her young friend's resolve.

"Is it truly that grand?"

"It is. Come, let us fix some tea and talk more, but do promise me that you will at least think on my words."

"I will think on them."

Miranda put an arm around Artemis for a quick squeeze. She felt triumphant at the fact that her dear young friend's affections were not deeply engaged. Although there remained some tension, Artemis was no longer at daggers drawn toward her. She softened considerably as they chatted about some of the gentlemen whose initials appeared on the other girls' hazelnuts. It was then that Miranda realized what Artemis needed. She needed to shine at the Shepeshed Ball.

In fact, Miranda wondered if Artemis' reasons for pursuing Evan were not tied to feelings of inadequacy. Spending time in the company of half a dozen dainty females could produce such an effect on one's confidence, especially when many of the diminutive young misses had also etched the letter A into their hazelnuts.

Miranda knew what she must do. She needed to show Artemis that she was a desirable young lady in her own right. Evan's cooperation would be a required ingredient to the success of her plan, if he would oblige her.

The next day brought milder air and sunshine. Many of the gentlemen were loath to let such a day go to waste indoors, and so they formed several hunting parties to go in search of grouse and pheasant.

That afternoon, Miranda tracked down Evan where she knew she would find him, in the stables. She entered in haste, not bothering to admire the sight of several cleaned pheasants hanging to cure. Neither did she notice that the stalls had been raked clean and scattered with fresh straw from the late summer's harvest. The earthy smell tickled

Miranda's nose, but she gave it no thought. She
had to find Evan. She was determined to gain his
help in making Artemis a success at the All Hallow's Eve Ball.

He stood near Castlestone, Rothwell's prime
hunter, stroking the mighty steed's nose. A ridiculous thought struck her as she watched man and
beast with their heads close together. They looked
almost as if they carried on a conversation, each one
commiserating with the troubles of the other.

"Is he any better?" Miranda asked, when she stood
before him.

Evan looked up quickly, as if caught in deep
thought. "Yes, but he is in no condition to hunt on
Monday. Two other stallions and a gelding belonging
to Rothwell are also ill with the same affliction."

"That is ghastly unfortunate."

"And costly," Evan added.

"How do you mean?"

"Rothwell cannot expect to sell sick horses at the
Quorn. He will lose out on several hundred pounds
this year, possibly even a thousand. Not that he
needs the blunt, but even so."

"I see." Miranda looked about. Stable boys were
busy cleaning stalls and polishing the tack. Saddles
gleamed in the sunlight that streamed in through
spotless windows. "Have you spoken to the groom?"

"I have. I told him about the man you saw that
night. At first he was concerned, and then he said
that it was most likely Gerald, who has been with
Rothwell for years. Gerald had been sent into the
stables that evening on an errand."

"But the cape," Miranda said.

"The cape is what distinguished him. The head
groom said he wears it often to chase away the chill

air. So it would seem there is no foul play there." He tapped the toe of his tasseled Hessians against the stall door.

Miranda absently petted Castlestone's neck. " 'Tis a good way to scuff your boots and make your valet angry."

Evan laughed, causing his dimples to crease his cheeks deeply. "Trust me, my valet is used to the state of my roughened clothes. I did not even have such a servant until Clasby rang a peal over my head. He said it was past time I looked the part of a titled landowner."

"You have always looked better than simply presentable, Evan," Miranda said softly. She was pleased to see his color deepen.

"We were young then, Miranda, and I had no idea how to go on."

"You were always a gentleman."

"I did not always wish to play the perfect gentleman, and you know it," he said with quiet intensity.

It was Miranda's turn to blush. She felt her cheeks grow hot. She knew exactly of what he spoke. He had pressured her and pleaded with her for more liberties than mere kisses. It had taken all her determination to keep herself pure, since he had been as accomplished as he was ardent.

She had often wondered what it would have been like had she made love with Evan. Would the memory of that physical act have given her comfort during her chaste life with Crandle? Or would it have been a source of constant regret?

She wanted to reach out and touch him; in fact he looked as if he'd welcome it, but she nearly trembled with fear. What if he rejected her yet again? Instead, she changed the subject back to the safe ground of the horses. "Do you think it simply a coincidence, the horses getting sick?"

The seductive spell that had been cast by their memories was effectively broken. Evan returned to a congenial, if wary, truce-abiding *friend*. "It is possible. They could have eaten the same plant or some such. But, still, I cannot help but wonder who might stand to gain from Rothwell not showing at the Quorn," he said.

"Would any of the guests be in such a position?"

"I cannot think so. I tend to believe that it is a neighboring lord."

"But who would be so cruel?"

"There is one man with a reputation for a nasty disposition within the hunting set. It is known that he envies Rothwell's talent in turning out prime hunters. But I have no proof, nothing to back up any claims I might make."

"Can you not speak with him?"

"Not unless I wish to be challenged to a duel."

Miranda reached out and laid her hand upon Evan's arm. "How utterly despicable. Please say that you would not meet this man should he challenge you."

He looked at her hand, then into her eyes. "I will not meet him. I've changed, Miranda. I have worked hard to leave the hot-headed man you once knew behind."

Miranda reluctantly pulled her hand back. "There were good things about that man too." A current of desire flowed between them. It was strong, it was tangible, and it was exhilarating. What if they were to kiss again with deliberate concentration? Her insides were molten at the mere thought. She glanced at his mouth and licked her lips.

"Did you wish to inquire after the horses, or was there another reason for you to venture once again into the stables?" he asked, as he moved down to the next stall, where his own hunter perked up its ears and raised its head. He put considerable distance between them to protect himself.

Miranda shook her head in an attempt to clear it and remember why she had searched him out. "I did indeed seek you on purpose." It was about Artemis. "I have a favor to ask of you."

"Indeed?" He raised his eyebrows.

"I would ask that you not dance more than once with Artemis this evening at the Shepeshed Ball."

"Why do you ask this of me?"

"For Artemis' sake. I wish her to be a shining success at the ball. This is her first real ball since coming out."

He looked confused by her request. "Can I not provide success by partnering her as a suitor?"

"Evan, if you hang about her all evening, you will chase away other gentlemen who might approach her."

"That would seem to be the wise thing to do, considering that I hope to make her my wife."

His intent stated in such a matter-of-fact manner chased the air from her lungs. It hurt more than she would have thought possible. Taking a moment to recover, she pressed on. "Artemis deserves some attention, which I am confident she will receive, based on the reaction of the young men at the fair. Evan, do you not see? If you send a clear message that she is *yours*, Artemis will never have the chance to shine on her own. She will be the envy of many a young lady, but that is all. The gentlemen will not come near her, and Artemis will continue to feel inadequate in comparison to the other young ladies."

"Go on. I follow you." He scratched his chin as he contemplated her words.

"It is being said that the only reason you show interest in Artemis is because you admire her father and her skill with horses. Artemis cannot be ignorant of the whispers. She needs one night of appreciation from other young gentlemen to prove her worth as a female. She certainly will not receive much of it if you hover about her."

"I see."

"I come to you as a friend"—she nearly choked on the word—"for the benefit of Artemis."

"And if she decides she wishes to wed another gentleman, what then? I will have lost a bride." His voice was soft, and there was a hint of a smile about his shapely lips, causing the dimples in his cheeks to tease her.

You could have me. The thought raced through her mind. "I have been completely honest in my opinion that the two of you do not suit. I have not changed my mind on that score. If she finds a man she can love, who truly loves her in return, then so much the better."

"For whom is it better?"

"For both of you," she said. *And for me.*

Chapter Ten

*E*van stood against the wall of the modestly appointed but large assembly rooms of Shepeshed. The place threatened to become a sad crush.
Open to all of local society, the gentry as well as the
nobility, the event saw the crowd mingle in relative
harmony.

He had done his duty, as Miranda had requested.
He danced only a demure cotillion with Artemis
early in the evening. When he left her, she had several dances already reserved. One of them with a
young puppy no older than twenty years. He did not
understand why he had agreed to Miranda's request,
other than from an urge to please her. It made no
sense to him. What difference did it make if Artemis
had a hundred dances with eligible men if, in the
end, she agreed to marry him?

He tapped the heel of his evening slipper against
the wall as he wrestled with unease for the second
time since he had decided to wed Artemis Rothwell.
Once he married Artemis, he'd spend the rest of his
life with her. He was not the type to engage the
services of a mistress to overcome what his wife
lacked in skill. The woman he wed would be the
only woman he'd bed.

He looked on as Artemis moved with lithe grace through the steps of a quadrille. She was fresh-faced and young and had her whole life waiting for her. He felt as if he had already lived half of his. Was Miranda correct about their unsuitability?

She appeared before him as if conjured up by his thoughts, and his pulse quickened immediately. It was difficult to keep his gaze upon her face. One glance at the deep plunge of her neckline, and his eyes automatically sought the generous swell of her breasts. The gown she wore fit her to perfection, and she looked every inch the name the *ton* had given her. She was indeed the "Portrait of Beauty."

"Good evening, Evan," she said with a brazen smile. She knew he had been admiring her décolletage.

"Miranda."

"Why are you not dancing?" She cocked an eyebrow.

"You asked that I partner Artemis only once."

"But there are other ladies present."

"I am not one for dancing."

"You used to be," she said.

It was true. He used to love to dance, especially with her. They had moved as one, as if their feet floated just above the dance floor. He wondered if they could still create such magic.

"Very well. May I have the next dance with you?" he asked.

"I should like that above all things," she said.

They stood next to one another in silence as they watched the quadrille and waited for it to end. When the strains of a waltz began, Evan regretted his decision. The waltz was far too intimate. Holding Miranda in his arms courted danger. The minx took his offered arm with a look of pure satisfaction, and he knew he was in grave trouble.

He led her out onto the ballroom floor and whirled her into his arms, careful to keep a proper distance between them. She offered him a challenging grin when he nervously placed his hand at the small of her back. He wondered if this had been her intent all along. By promising not to dance more than once with Artemis, Evan had been left entirely too free to dance with Miranda.

He could not deny that Miranda had lost much of the haughty reserve she had exhibited when he first arrived. A welcome warmth spilled from her, tempting him to get closer and revel in the heat. Any physical contact with her was enough to drive him to distraction, and waltzing with her was no exception. He did his best to control the urge to draw her closer.

He had agreed to become her friend. Since doing so, he was surprised that he actually enjoyed her company, even though he battled the attraction he felt for her. If anything, the attraction had grown even more intense. He knew she had wanted him to kiss her earlier in the stables this afternoon. It had taken considerable determination to move away from her.

He was not about to stop controlling his desire for her with an iron will. He could not be what he had once been all those years ago. He was not about to become a London gentleman in order to please her. He'd not live in her pocket, either.

He had been so desperately in love with her all those years ago that he had literally lost himself in her. He would have done or given up anything for her. That depth of desire shook him to the very core. With it came an insane jealousy that had torn up his peace. When he was not with her, he wondered who it was that she spoke to, what gentlemen called upon her. It had been sheer torture. He refused to repeat history. He was better off with Artemis.

"You are quiet," Miranda said, breaking into his thoughts. They circled the outer rim of dancers. "Is something wrong?"

"No, nothing at all." He tried to relax, but her hand burned in his own.

"Evan, really, you look as if you are afraid of me," she teased.

"Perhaps I am." At the glimpse of her low neckline, he became deadly serious in an instant. Until this night, she had dressed with the utmost modesty appropriate for the country. The gown she wore tonight belonged in the ballrooms and salons of London. Sophistication dripped from her, along with confidence in her appearance. She would never be satisfied with a life spent at his home in the Derbyshire countryside.

She boldly stared into his eyes, as if daring him to do something about his obvious appreciation of her charms. She was no green girl; she had been married for seven years. In the depths of her gaze, he read her invitation to be far more than mere friends, and he was sorely tempted. He found himself heeding her call as if he had no will of his own. He pulled her closer and was lost in the heat of her and the music.

They moved with grace, sweeping around other couples in time to the music. They did not speak the rest of the dance; they did not have to. They gazed into each other's eyes as they swayed, and Evan did not think again of their past. He simply savored this moment, knowing it would be one of their last together.

Miranda saw the sadness creep into Evan's eyes and wondered what he was thinking. She did not even try to deny the fact that she wanted him like no other. She decided there and then that she would do all she could to have him. After seven long years, she would finally pursue her heart's desire. And what her heart wanted most of all was Evan Langley, Earl of Ashbourne. She wanted his love once again.

When the waltz ended, and Evan bowed before her, she felt bereft. She knew he fought against his attraction for her, but she did not understand why. What was so terrible about her that he feared the desire they shared? It was ridiculous to think that he was actually afraid of her.

"Shall we make for the refreshment table?" he asked.

"By all means." She followed him through the crowded rooms until they reached the area set aside for punch and various cakes. It was there that they found Miss Whitlow comforting a visibly pale Artemis.

Miranda reached out to touch Artemis' arm. "What is it, my dear? What has happened?"

Artemis looked up with hurt-filled eyes. "It is nothing." She tried to hide behind a brave smile, but when she saw Evan, her lower lip trembled. "I beg your pardon, do excuse me." Artemis nearly ran across the crowded floor to the private room set aside for the ladies.

Evan's expression was grim. "What is it?"

"I do not know," Miranda said. "Miss Whitlow, what has happened?"

"Some of the gentlemen are in their cups and have been saying cruel things."

"Like what?" Evan's deep voice remained soft, but it threatened like the sound of distant thunder.

"Simply that she is no goddess; she is merely a giantess who can ride and aim like a man," Miss Whitlow explained. "Artemis tried to pay such remarks little heed, but when Lord Ranton, a gentleman she particularly favored, asked one of the Waterton-Smythe sisters to dance, Artemis overheard him make cutting remarks about her stature. The two of them compared her to a horse. I think that was the comment that cut her to the quick. She thinks she is plain as it is."

"Where is this gentleman?" Evan asked, with a determined glint in his eye.

Miranda laid a hand upon his arm. "Do not call more attention to the matter; it will only serve to embarrass Artemis further. Thank you, Miss Whitlow, do run along. I see that your partner for the cotillion is waiting."

"Thank you, Lady Crandle." The young lady dashed off.

Miranda looked up into Evan's serious eyes. "I shall seek her out and see what can be done to bring her back with her head held high."

She turned to follow where Artemis had gone, but Evan delayed her. "We can remedy the situation by having her dance with me," he said, in a tone that broached no argument.

"Yes, perhaps that would help." She patted his hand distractedly. She had to find Artemis.

"Miranda, she would not have been subjected to such cruelty if she had been firmly established as my intended this evening."

That stopped her cold. She turned to face him,

carefully choosing her words. "That is not quite true. Such things might still have been said. People often choose to be cruel, no matter how high-bred their victim."

"You speak from experience?" he asked quietly.

"As a matter of fact, I do. You cannot imagine what was said of me considering Crandle's age and wealth."

"I beg your pardon. I should have guessed."

"You could not have known. You were never in London." Bitterness had seeped into her voice. She had often looked for him, hoping simply to see him. Year after year, her hopes had been dashed.

"I had my reasons for staying away."

"Me," she stated.

"Yes, you. What would you have had me do? If I saw you with Crandle . . ." He did not bother to finish.

Miranda felt the heat of irritation rise to her cheeks. It was neither the time nor the place to discuss the matter. But even so, she could not believe he had kept clear of London simply because she was there. "We were speaking of Artemis," she reminded him.

"Yes, we were. Having my interest publicly displayed might have protected her. You cannot deny it."

Frustrated, Miranda did not answer for fear she would perhaps later regret her words. With tight lips, she said, "I must go to her. I shall speak more on the matter with you later." Miranda hurried away from him into the private parlor.

Evan watched her go. Why did everything turn to what had happened between them? It was time he closed that chapter of his life for good and stop holding it over her head every chance he could. He understood Miranda's reasons for marrying Crandle. He did not fault her, so why could he not be done with the whole thing and leave it alone?

He shook his head and walked back to the ballroom. He'd seek out this rude young blood and give him a thing to think about.

"What has Lady Crandle running from you as fast as her feet will carry her?" Clasby asked.

Evan was so lost in his thoughts about Miranda that he had not even noticed Clasby approach him. "One of the young men here insulted Miss Rothwell. Miranda is going to comfort her. I plan to have words with the fellow. Care to join me?"

Clasby narrowed his gaze with that all-too-familiar expression. Clasby was seeing through him again, weighing Evan's actions against what he said. Clasby always looked for deep truths beneath the surface. But he merely said, "Lead on, old boy."

Miranda stepped into the spacious parlor filled with scattered vanities and privacy stalls. She was grateful that it was empty save for the two of them. She spied Artemis at the far vanity, alternately pinching her cheeks and wiping her nose. Miranda pulled out a chair next to her and sat down. "Are you feeling better?"

"I am a fool," Artemis said softly.

Miranda grabbed hold of her hand and gave it a squeeze. "You are not, dear. Why ever would you say so?"

"I have been mincing about as if I belong. I have only made myself look ridiculous." She pulled out her handkerchief and blew her nose with a hearty honk. Then she crumpled the sodden linen into a ball and shoved it into her reticule. Her eyes still threatened a tear or two, and she continued to sniffle.

"One man's comments do not represent the opinion of many." Miranda pulled out her own handkerchief and handed it to Artemis.

"Thank you," she said with a watery laugh. "It is no use, Miranda. I am a hatchet-faced giant."

"You are far from plain. You are positively regal in your God-blessed stature. If some of the local bucks are too blind to see that, then you shall simply have to come to London, where I will prove it to you. There they have a more discerning eye."

Artemis gave a bitter little laugh. "He was from London." She shook her head. "It does not matter. I am resigned to the fact that I am what I am. I will never cut a dash, as do the other young ladies. I am sorry, Miranda. I know you chose Ashbourne to be on your hazelnut too, but I must accept him and be done with it. I have to leave someday; it may as well be with a prime catch that will make my father proud."

Miranda fought to control the swell of panic that overwhelmed her. Artemis could not accept the first man to ask for her hand, simply because her father approved. She felt incredibly protective of her dear friend's daughter but also exasperated with her. "Artemis Rothwell," she scolded, "think what you are saying!"

Artemis blew her nose again.

"Beatrice did not raise you to give up so easily or to feel sorry for yourself." Miranda stood and held out her hand. "Now, come with me. You must hold your head high and dance and enjoy the rest of your evening."

Artemis tilted her chin stubbornly. "You cannot

even begin to understand how I feel. You are beautiful and accomplished. I can never be you, so please stop trying to make me into something I am not. Stop trying to make me into you. I should have been a boy; then everyone would just leave me alone to do whatever I wanted."

Miranda's self-righteous indignation vanished in an instant. It was true. She was indeed trying to change Artemis. She believed that Artemis deserved a love match, because Miranda had wanted one. And much as Crandle had done to her when she was young, Miranda had tried to refine Artemis as if the person she truly was inside had no appeal.

"Artemis, I humbly beg your pardon." She sat back down. "I love you, dearest. I would not hurt you for the world."

"I know that; truly I do."

"But you cannot settle, even for Evan, a 'prime catch.' What is it that you truly want?" Miranda asked.

"If I knew that, it would not be so difficult, now would it?" Artemis asked with a soft laugh.

Miranda realized that she should in fact heed her own words. If she wanted a life with Evan, she could not allow Artemis' hurt feelings to sway her resolve. Artemis did not love Evan. She was only considering his suit because it pleased her father and because he was a prize that would give her great pride to catch.

Nor could she wait for Evan to change his mind about her. He not only did not know his own heart, he was afraid of it. But she knew her own. She was not going to settle for anything less than winning Evan's love once again.

Evan looked about the room. "There's that Ranton fellow, over there," he said. "He's hanging about with Osbaldeston's set. No wonder he's a good-for-nothing."

Clasby placed a hand upon his arm. "Easy, Ashbourne, don't go starting something you'll need help finishing. I'm no good as a second in a duel, and I'm pretty certain that Rothwell would not approve."

"There are some things Rothwell need not know," Evan said, but he pondered Clasby's warning. If he did in fact confront Ranton, and the cub was as bad as the crew he ran with, then a duel would indeed be probable.

"What does that mean?" Clasby asked. "You know he'd find out eventually."

"Yes, yes. You are right, of course." He thought of the fear in Miranda's eyes when he mentioned the possibility of a duel with Osbaldeston. "Look," he said to Clasby, "I think someone may be tampering with Rothwell's horses. In my opinion, the most likely culprit is Osbaldeston. He has the most to gain if Rothwell's hunters have a bad showing."

"I see what you mean," Clasby said. "You have not told Rothwell?"

"No, I could not be sure, and the horses appear to be improving. I've told only Miranda."

Clasby fingered his chin. "Ah yes, the fair Lady Crandle. You have been often in her company these last two days."

Evan felt prickly and defensive. "So?"

"For whom do you play the knight errant?" Clasby asked. "Miss Rothwell, the gel you offered for; her father, whom you admire; or the fair Lady Crandle, who quite dotes on Miss Rothwell, as well as on you?"

Evan gave him a sharp look. The three of them were connected and equally slandered by the remark made by Ranton: Miranda, because she had done her best to help Artemis out of her awkwardness, Rothwell, because it was his daughter, and, of course, Artemis, who had been insulted. "What does it matter?"

"Take a good look at the reasons you wish to protect them, and then you'll know why it matters."

"Clasby, you talk in riddles."

"Perhaps. But there is always an answer of profound truth behind a mere riddle." He gave him a slap upon the back.

Evan rubbed his forehead. It throbbed. Perhaps it would be best if he left it alone for now. The evening was almost over. He need not make a spectacle by taking the young lord to task in front of his cronies. There'd be time later on or at the Quorn to speak his piece if need be. "Very well, let us back down for now."

"A good choice, considering that your fair Miranda is bearing down upon you with Miss Rothwell in tow."

Evan turned. Miranda was indeed coming toward him. He thought about Clasby's riddle. For whom *did* he act the knight errant?

"Good evening, Mr. Clasby," Miranda said. "I do believe this is our dance."

"Indeed it is," Clasby said, quickly picking up on her lead. "I had almost forgotten." Clasby extended his arm.

"I shall leave Artemis in your capable hands, Ashbourne." She gave him a pointed look. It was his turn to mend the situation.

Evan bowed and offered Artemis his arm. He had just been instructed to dance with her. "Miss Rothwell?" he asked. "Shall we join the dance?"

"I should like that above all things," she replied.

He escorted Artemis onto the floor and joined another couple to make up a set of four. As they bobbed and weaved through the steps, he kept glancing toward Miranda and Clasby. Miranda laughed at something Clasby had said, and jealousy stabbed his insides.

"Is something wrong, Ashbourne?" Artemis asked.

Evan dragged his attention back to Artemis. "Nothing at all."

"You looked quite grim just now as you watched Mr. Clasby with Lady Crandle." She narrowed her eyes as she looked at him. "I understand that you knew Lady Crandle during her Season."

Evan felt his throat go dry. "Yes." They exchanged partners with the couple in their set.

When they came back together, Artemis looked at him with shrewd eyes. "Did you love her?"

She was far too bold for her own good, he thought. "It was many years ago." He did not wish to discuss the past love of his life with his new intended.

They met in the middle of the square they had made with the other couple. With hands held high, they circled counterclockwise. "I see," she said. With firm determination in her eyes, she addressed him directly. "Ashbourne," she began, "I have given it much thought, and I would like to accept your kind offer. I think we shall suit quite well."

Evan almost tripped over his own feet. It was the answer he had wanted, and yet it took him by surprise. In fact, he felt a twinge of fear. He recovered quickly since she awaited his response. "I am honored." He bowed his head, trying to think of something else to say. But Artemis appeared to be satisfied as they swapped partners once again, and she smiled.

When the dance came to an end, Evan led Artemis to her parents, who looked ready to leave the gathering. Several of the others in the Rothwell party were heading to the anteroom to retrieve their outer garments as well. The carriages were being brought around.

"We are calling it a night," Rothwell said.

"A wise decision," Evan said. "Clasby and I shall remain a bit longer, just to get a feel of who's riding come Monday. Take the measure of our competition."

"What's that?" Clasby had joined them. Miranda wore her pelisse. Her hands were stuffed inside a large black muff.

"I thought we could make inquiries about our competition on Monday," Evan explained. The truth of the matter is that he did indeed wish to speak to Ranton and find out what he knew of Osbaldeston's hunters. He also thought he had seen a tavern in town. He felt the need for something a bit stronger than the weak wine punch that had been served.

"Do be careful," Miranda said, quickly adding, "I mean, on the way home."

Miranda paced the floor of her bedchamber, worried about Evan. His room was just down the hall from hers, and she hoped she would hear his footsteps when he came home. After they left the assembly rooms, she feared he would look for trouble in addition to seeking information that might shed light upon the reason that Rothwell's hunters were sick. She imagined all sorts of terrible happenings, from an outright brawl to a challenge of pistols at dawn.

When she heard soft footfalls well past one o'clock in the morning, she rushed to her door and peeked out. It was indeed Evan. He was standing practically in front of her, as if considering whether to knock upon her door.

"Is all well?" she whispered.

"What are you doing still awake?" he whispered back.

"You stopped outside my door—were you planning to knock?"

"Of course not." He looked offended. With a Gallic shrug and slight smile bringing out those seductive dimples, he asked, "May I come in?"

She opened the door to him, a shiver of anticipation running along her spine. What did he want? She felt painfully aware of him as he walked by her. He smelled slightly of smoke and brandy. Clasby's cheroots again!

This was her bedchamber, and they were alone, and it was late. No one would ever know if he stayed with her until morning. She shook her head. Compromising him was no way to capture his heart, even if no one cared now she was a widow. But Evan would care, and, in the end, so would she.

"What did you wish to speak with me about?" she asked, her voice sounding loud and nervous to her ears.

"I wanted to beg your forgiveness," he said.

"Whatever for?"

"I blamed you for what happened to Artemis this evening, and that was not in the least fair."

Miranda blinked. Warmth spread through her at the softness of his words, making her bare toes curl into the carpet under her feet. She did not know what to say.

"I spoke to Ranton." Evan cleared his throat. "He is the young lord who insulted Artemis to one of the

Waterton-Smythe sisters. He's a ne'er-do-well rogue in training. I think Osbaldeston is his idol. Ranton's well on his way to that level of cruelty."

"I have met Lord Osbaldeston in town, and I was not in the least impressed with the man. Do not say he is the neighboring lord you think might have tampered with Rothwell's horses!"

"The very same."

"What did this Ranton fellow have to say? Did he shed any light upon the situation?"

"No." Evan padded across the floor and sat upon the sofa near the fireplace.

Miranda took a seat across from him. "Then, what happened?"

"Ranton knew about the sick horses. I'd bet a monkey it was Osbaldeston's doing somehow, but, again, I have no proof." Evan ran a hand through his short dark hair, making it stand up on end.

Miranda restrained herself from smoothing his disordered shorn locks back into place. "I do thank you for coming to me with your kind apology," she said softly.

Evan looked uncomfortable and he quickly stood. He also looked hesitant to leave, as if he had something on his mind, something else he wished to say.

She stood as well. On impulse she reached out and took hold of his hand. She wanted to keep him from leaving if she could, and she simply wanted to touch him. "I must also thank you for coming to Artemis' rescue by dancing with her that last dance. She held her head high as she took her leave."

He said nothing but brought her hand to his lips for a tender kiss that nearly brought her to her knees. She was weak with need and longing for him and feared that she might just throw herself at his feet and beg him to stay. "If you still intend to wed Artemis," Miranda said, in an emotion-ragged whisper, "you had best leave now."

He released her hand in an instant. "Of course," he said stiffly. "I had no business coming here like this. I beg your pardon."

"But I am glad that you did." Miranda walked him to the door, her heart beating wildly in her chest. She felt deep disappointment, but she knew she could not allow him to stay, not under Beatrice's roof.

Miranda also knew all too well that if she made love to Evan, she would indeed be destroyed if he decided afterward that he did not want her. Silently, she opened the door and looked out to make sure no one was in the hall. "Good evening, then," she said.

He stepped out into the hall. He looked as if he wished to say something more, but instead he briefly caressed her cheek and whispered, "Sleep well, Miranda."

Miranda closed her door and leaned against it. As tears of frustration spilled silently down her cheeks, she slid down to sit upon the floor, hugging her knees against her chest. How could she prove to Evan that they belonged together?

Chapter Eleven

*E*arly the next morning, Evan made his way to the stables to check on the horses. He cursed himself for not telling Miranda that Artemis had accepted him. He had tried to form the words but each time they had stuck in his throat, where they remained unsaid.

Once inside the stable, he looked over each horse and found that every horse belonging to a guest of Rothwell's remained healthy. Only Rothwell's three prized hunters had experienced any colic. More than ever, he believed Osbaldeston was behind this misfortune.

He stroked the neck of Castlestone, Artemis' favorite. The horse had improved, but not to the extent that he could be ridden on the morrow in the Quorn. Rothwell's horses were out of the hunt.

He drew near to his own horse, pleased that he remained healthy. Tomorrow was the opening of the Quorn. Evan felt the thrill of anticipated excitement rush along his spine. He planned to stay throughout the week and then return home to his estate duties.

One of those duties was finding a wife in order to set up his nursery. He absently stroked the mane of his hunter, battling with doubts. He wondered if offering for Artemis Rothwell so soon was the wisest course. He had not spent nearly enough time with her to know for sure, and now he regretted the precipitousness of his actions. Had he not been trying so hard to escape from his feelings for Miranda, he might have trod more slowly, more carefully.

"Ah, Ashbourne. An early riser like myself," Rothwell said from behind him.

Evan nearly jumped. He had not heard him enter the stables.

"I do hope you plan to attend church service with us this morning." Rothwell's voice boomed, making Evan almost wince. It had been so quiet just moments ago.

"Yes, certainly." Evan had not considered church, but judging by the expression on Rothwell's face, he dared not refuse.

"Good." Rothwell slapped him on the back. "You'll sit with us in the family pew"—Rothwell winked—"since you will soon be a part of us. Artemis has told me that she will accept your offer of marriage." Rothwell extended his hand. "Congratulations are in order."

Evan numbly extended his hand. It was as good as done. Artemis Rothwell had agreed to become his wife.

Evan remained standing in the middle of the stable long after Rothwell had left, when Clasby walked in.

"What is wrong with you?" Clasby asked.

"Nothing." Evan turned back toward his horse. It was what he wanted, what he had intended when he came here, but he felt deeply dissatisfied.

"How is your horse, is he fit?"

"Completely. My replacements are fine as well. As are all the guest's horses."

"So you still think Osbaldeston is behind this?"

"You heard Ranton. He raved that Osbaldeston's horses would show the best this year. How is it that Ranton knew Rothwell's three prized hunters were sick? Not one of the mares or any of the other horses suffers from illness. I tell you, someone has been tampering, and I'll wager it was Osbaldeston. I will get to the bottom of it."

"How?"

"I do not quite know that yet. I may have to confront Osbaldeston."

Clasby shifted from foot to foot. "Do you truly think it will do any good? He might call you out."

"I cannot simply let it go."

"I suppose not," Clasby agreed. "Do you plan to attend church this morning?"

"Yes," Evan sighed. He needed to have a serious conversation with this Gerald fellow whom Miranda had spied upon. "Will Lady Crandle be attending?" he asked quickly.

"I imagine so," Clasby said. "Does it matter?"

"Not in the least." Evan did not relish facing Miranda this morning. He remembered too clearly the sweetness of her expression last night when he was in her chamber. She had been all too willing if he had made a move toward her. It had taken considerable self-restraint to leave her rooms. He was glad that he had. It would have been much more difficult to face her with the news of Artemis' agreement to wed him had he kissed her again.

"You still have feelings for her," Clasby said quietly.

Evan jerked his head up. "Nonsense," he said too quickly.

"With the 'Portrait of Beauty' within your grasp, why would you settle for a young miss who obviously does not move you?"

"It is because she does not move me that I remain safe," Evan said softly.

"What in Hades are you talking about?" Clasby asked, looking concerned.

Evan shook his head. "Nothing. Look, it is as good as done. Rothwell said that Artemis has accepted me."

Clasby whistled through his teeth. "Are you sure about this?"

Evan ignored him. "What time does church services start?"

"In two hours. You have time to break your fast and change."

"Very well. I shall see you in church."

Soft overcast light streamed through the stained glass of the Rothwell parish chapel. Miranda watched the dust motes dance in the rainbow-colored rays when the sun peeped out from behind a cloud to shine in upon them. It was difficult to pay attention to the curate as he preached his sermon.

The topic was God's truth being found in the most unlikely places, but she paid little attention. Her gaze often rested on Evan's broad shoulders, encased in dark green superfine, while her heart twisted inside her breast.

He sat with the Rothwells in their family pew as if he belonged there, and that worried her. She did not miss the smug smile upon Rothwell's face when Evan took his seat next to Artemis. Nor did Miranda miss the panicked glance Beatrice cast toward her. Something had changed. Artemis would not even look at her.

Miranda watched Evan throughout the service. He sat stiffly next to Artemis, his back straight as a board. Although they shared a hymnal book for the concluding hymn, Evan kept his distance from Artemis. He did not allow even their shoulders to touch.

The service ended, and Miranda followed the others out into the brisk air. She was astonished to find Mr. Clasby on her heels. "Good morning, Mr. Clasby," she said, when he nearly bumped into her.

He bowed with a grin. "Lady Crandle. You are looking your finest this morning."

"Thank you, sir." She knew he fibbed since the darkness under her eyes bespoke a restless night. "I must own that I am surprised to see you in church."

"How so?"

"I thought you said you were not a church-going man."

"Ah, but when in Rome . . ."

Miranda laughed. "I am indeed glad Evan has a friend like you," she said recklessly. "You must give him the light-hearted balance that he needs."

Mr. Clasby looked taken aback by her compliment but pleased all the same. He moved closer and lowered his voice to a whisper. "It is you, dear lady, whom he needs. And that is my not-so-humble opinion."

Miranda felt a flush of warmth wash over her. She reached out and clasped Mr. Clasby's hand. "I think so too." She had an ally, and that bolstered her lagging spirits considerably.

Evan did not miss the exchange between Clasby

and Miranda, and it made his blood boil. He suppressed the urge to interrupt them. It did not matter any longer. He was as good as betrothed. Whatever Miranda chose to do and with whom could no longer be permitted to draw his attention. Even so, he felt engulfed by a red haze of jealous anger. He could not look away from the pair of them. Now that Clasby knew which way was up, he needed no excuse to stay away from Miranda. She was fair game.

He did not want her for himself, so why should he begrudge her the chance to find another? Would she decide to pursue Clasby once she heard of his betrothal? He knew Miranda would not be pleased in the least, but would she fall into Clasby's arms to ease her disappointment?

The thought nearly made him sick.

"Ashbourne?" Artemis pulled at his arm like the child he was beginning to see that she was.

"Yes?" His patience was teetering upon the edge of a steep cliff. *What had he bloody done?*

"What has you looking like a thundercloud?"

He forced a smile as he looked into the dark and eager eyes of Artemis Rothwell. She was a dear young lady, but it was true; she was perhaps too young. He felt his cravat tighten about his throat. "Nothing. The sun is simply shining in my eyes."

Luncheon was served promptly in the dining room after they returned from the Rothwell chapel. Miranda tried to speak with Beatrice, but her dear friend bustled about arranging and then rearranging the seating assignments.

"Bea?" Miranda asked.

"Yes, dear?" Beatrice did not look up. She continued to place the elegant cards upon the table in front of each chair.

"A rather formal meal, is it not?" Something in her friend's manner disturbed her. Something was indeed wrong.

"It is Sunday." Beatrice finally looked up, and then she quickly focused on her task.

Miranda nodded. "What has happened? Is it Artemis?"

Beatrice ignored the question entirely. "Could you check with Cook on the syllabub? She was having trouble with it, and I know you have a flair for making it."

"Certainly." Miranda rushed to do her bidding, only to find that Cook had mixed the sweetened cream and white wine to perfection. By the time she had returned to the dining room, the guests had all taken their seats. There was no time to find out what was troubling Beatrice.

Throughout the meal, the men chattered with fevered excitement about the hunt. Miranda ate sparingly, as she looked from Evan to Artemis sitting oddly silent next to one another.

After the sweetmeats and nuts were brought around, the footmen placed champagne and syllabub in front of each guest. And Rothwell rose at the end of the table.

"I have some proud news to share," Rothwell said. A hush fell across the room. All heads were turned in their host's direction.

Miranda noticed that Beatrice stared at her with an apologetic smile. Suddenly, Miranda knew what Rothwell was about to say, and dread filled her. She sat still as a statue, waiting for the news she did not wish to hear.

"My daughter has agreed to Lord Ashbourne's suit. I am proud to announce the betrothal of my dear Artemis and to propose a toast to their happiness." Rothwell raised his cup.

A round of applause filled the room, but Miranda heard none of it. She clapped as one should in such circumstances, but she had no goodwill to impart. She looked at Evan, who smiled and nodded to those who congratulated him. Artemis did the same. Even the Waterton-Smythe sister bounced out of their chairs to bestow their best wishes on Artemis. She would soon become a countess.

"I am so sorry, my dear," Beatrice whispered next to her ear.

Miranda sat frozen in her seat.

"Beldon made me promise not to say a word; he wanted it to be a surprise." Beatrice pressed her shoulder comfortingly.

"It is that," Miranda managed. But it was no real surprise to her. Evan had done what he came here to do. She only wished that Artemis had considered her choices before plunging ahead with an acceptance. She had also hoped that Evan might reconsider his plans after visiting her rooms the previous night. It appeared that all she had said to both of them had been for naught. Evan Langley, Earl of Ashbourne, and Artemis Rothwell were to be wed.

"Evan, may I speak with you?" Miranda asked, over the din of activity in the stables. It was well after dinner, and most of the guests had retired early in order to rise with the sun on the morrow.

Evan gritted his teeth. He had avoided her all day, but he knew that she'd seek him out eventually.

There was no escaping her. "What is it that you want?"

She ran her finger along the side of a stall, as if choosing her words carefully. His gaze stayed riveted on the tiny circles she made with her fingertips upon the wood. He imagined too clearly how her delicate fingers would feel on his skin.

"I must own that I was extremely disappointed with Rothwell's announcement today," she said.

He'd much rather leave it alone. He did not wish to speak of it to her. He had asked permission to pay his addresses to Artemis. He had been accepted by Rothwell and his daughter. It was part of the reason he had come to Rothwell Park. He did not want to admit that his doubts had come too late. Much too late. He was honor-bound to see the thing through.

"Miranda, it is why I came here." He busied himself with checking the tack for the horses he and his groom would take to the hunt tomorrow morning. The groom and other stable hands were also making ready for the eight-mile trek to Quorn.

She stepped toward him, her eyes pleading. "But it is completely wrong. Neither of you will be happy." She looked down then, and her voice quieted. "I thought that perhaps, in time, we might . . ."

"Pick up where we left off?" he asked with a cruel edge to his voice.

"Is that so wrong?" she asked in return. The stable hands ceased in their work, looking uneasy at her outburst.

He stood straighter, and with a nod of his head, they scattered, leaving the stable empty but for the two of them. "No." His lips curled. "It did not take long for you to find a replacement, as I had expected. Clasby will not deny you." His voice dripped contempt. He felt it all over again, the coiling tension he experienced all those years ago when another man looked at her. He hated this wildness of thought, this sensation of no control. For this reason alone, he would not let himself love her again.

She gasped as if she had been slapped. "What do you mean by that? Mr. Clasby has nothing to do with this."

He stepped closer. "I saw the two of you flirting this morning. For shame, Miranda, and right outside the church steps."

"What are you talking about?"

The madness took over, and he let it. It did not matter any more; his fate was sealed. He might as well let his anger have it's due. "How many men, Miranda? How many have there been? What difference does it make if you lose one? There are many willing to take my place, yet again. The "Portrait of Beauty" is a coveted prize. I did not have to visit London to know that much."

Fury and deep hurt shone from her eyes. "I cannot believe this. Evan, what is wrong with you?"

"You. *You* are what is wrong with me. You bring out the worst in me." There, he had said it. He had finally told her, not in the softest words he could have used, but at least his message was clear. He regretted it when he saw the tears well up in her eyes. He had wounded her deeply.

"Is this why you stayed away from London all these years? You feared your reaction to me?" she asked softly, fighting for composure.

All the fight went out of him in a moment of despair. "Yes."

"And now you seek Artemis' hand, whom you do not love. Why, Evan?" Her eyes sought his.

"Because with her I am in control."

She digested this information with quiet dignity. She did not rant nor burst into tears. She responded to his jealous ravings with utmost maturity, and he envied her for it. He felt like the lowest of cads. He had willingly hurt her because he could not control his own raging emotions. The fault was entirely his.

"Evan," she began. "Let me explain something to you, and then I shall forever leave you in peace. Crandle did not love me nor did he wish for an heir. I never understood why he schemed to marry me if he only wished to add me to his personal possessions. He protected me as if I was made of glass, but he never cherished me. He never even touched me."

Shock registered through him. How could the man not touch his own wife? Crandle was not ailing or decrepit; in fact, he was rather a fit older gentleman of good stature. "Why tell me this?"

"Because, everyday for seven years I regretted my decision. I came away from that marriage with absolutely nothing."

"You have a title and wealth," he offered quietly.

"Paltry substitutes, I assure you." She lifted her chin. "Do not offer Artemis these same things and think they are enough. Perhaps children might satisfy for a time, but even they cannot fill the hole of knowing your husband does not care one whit about you."

What could he say? He had no idea of how it had been for her. A vision of her hesitancy to eat the pudding at the picnic blurred in his mind's eye. Crandle had made sure that his prized "Portrait of

Beauty" remained just that. The realization of what she had been through humbled him.

"Crandle molded you into a trophy he could take pride in." He finally understood.

"We had a relationship of sorts, but it was nothing like it should have been. I was watched, and I was restricted in where I went, what I did, and even what I ate. I lacked for nothing, yet it was no life. It was no marriage."

He reached out to cup her chin, and caressed her cheek. "I beg your pardon. I did not realize."

"I thought of you so often that it hurt," she whispered, leaning into him. "I looked for you at every function, every Season. I read every gossip column in the Morning Post for news of you, and still I came away with nothing."

Warning bells sounded in his head, but he ignored them. He wanted one last taste of her. Just one. He would heed Miranda's words and do what he could to bring contentment to his marriage. He would do his best to be a good husband to Artemis. But he needed to say good-bye to Miranda properly.

He lowered his lips to softly brush against Miranda's lush mouth, and he was set adrift on a sea of longing. With a groan, he pulled her to him and deepened the kiss instantly.

Miranda clung to Evan as her heart shattered into a thousand pieces. He was making the biggest mistake of his life, she knew, because she had made the very same one seven years ago.

She returned his kiss with everything she felt for him, hoping to convey the depth of her love. She loved him, she had always loved him, and she was going to lose him yet again.

Stroking his face and crisp hair, she did not want

to let go of him. But he pulled back, he grabbed her hands to still them as he pushed her away, and that's when she heard the noise.

She turned in time as Evan ran toward the stable door calling out, "Artemis, wait." And then he was gone.

Miranda paced outside of Artemis' door, pleading with her, "Please, dear, open this door and let me explain."

"Never," came the muffled response.

Miranda let out a heavy sigh, her nerves stretched to the breaking point. She would have to go to Beatrice and tell her what had happened. She only hoped that Evan had gone to Rothwell. What a mess, she thought. She had never wanted to hurt Artemis through this whole affair, and she had just succeeded in doing so in the worst possible way.

She hurried down the hall to Beatrice and Rothwell's private apartments. It was indeed late when she knocked on the door.

A bleary-eyed Beatrice opened the door, "Miranda! Good heaven's, what time is it?"

"Half past eleven," Miranda said quietly. "I must talk to you."

Beatrice rubbed her eyes and stepped out into the hall, softly shutting the door behind her. "Let us go to your room, then."

Miranda wrung her hands the whole way. She feared Beatrice's reaction and censure. "Come in," she said, when they reached her room. "You will want to sit down."

Miranda continued to pace slowly, formulating her speech, her apology.

"Miranda, what is it? What troubles you so?"

"I have done a terrible thing, and I fear you may never forgive me." She stopped and knelt down by Beatrice's feet. "I am in love with your daughter's intended."

Beatrice stroked Miranda's hair. "I know, dear."

"Does it show?" she asked surprised.

"To me it does. I have suspected as much for a couple of days. I am so terribly sorry about all of this. Beldon is so proud he would not listen to me when I told him to hold off on any announcements."

Miranda shook her head. "No, that is not why I woke you. I am afraid that—" She paused, taking a deep breath. "—Artemis came upon Evan and me in the stables." She closed her eyes, ashamed. "We were kissing."

Beatrice's hand stilled. "When was this?"

"Not thirty minutes ago." Miranda opened her eyes to look into the face of her dearest friend. "I humbly beg your forgiveness. I never intended that Artemis should be hurt."

Beatrice held up her hand. "I know; truly, I do. Rothwell and I might have been too hasty. I will talk to Artemis, and no doubt Beldon will want to speak to Ashbourne."

Miranda sank down to sit upon the floor. She should have known that Beatrice would take some of the blame onto herself. "It is not your fault, Bea; it is mine. I have tried to talk to Artemis, but she will not hear a word from me."

"Where is she?" Beatrice asked.

"In her bedchamber."

Beatrice let out a heavy sigh before looking closely at Miranda. "Do you truly love Ashbourne?"

"With all of my heart."

"Does he love you in return?" Beatrice asked.

Miranda sat quietly. Evan had never professed any feelings for her other than complete frustration and the desire to be far away from her. "I do not know," she whispered.

Beatrice looked concerned. No doubt she did not like the idea of Evan playing fast and loose with Miranda when he had offered for Artemis. "What if he does not wish to withdraw his offer, Miranda? If Artemis still wishes to proceed with the betrothal, and Ashbourne does not object, what then?"

Tears sprang to Miranda's eyes. It was entirely possible that their embrace in the stables would not change a thing. "Then I shall go home and die." She knew she was being melodramatic, and yet that was how she felt. The part of her that had come to life had begun to dry up and wither again since the announcement had been made. If Evan did not want her, she could not remain at Rothwell Park. It would simply hurt too much to watch the two of them.

Beatrice rose to her feet, reaching down to pull Miranda up in order to embrace her soundly. "Do not fret anymore this night. I will try and talk to Artemis, but it may have to wait until tomorrow, when everyone's emotions have had a chance to cool."

Miranda held on tight. "Beatrice, you are far too good a friend to me."

"Nonsense." Beatrice pulled back and smiled. "I want only what is best for everyone. Artemis is young; she will recover. But you, my dear. It is for you that I worry."

Miranda nodded, too overcome to trust herself to speak. She walked Beatrice to the door and then closed it when she had gone. She burst into tears and sobbed until she was spent.

Chapter Twelve

Miranda woke to the sound of men's laughter in the halls. It was Monday morning, the opening of the Quorn. Miranda threw back the covers and sat on the edge of her bed, rubbing her eyes. She had tossed and turned for several hours before finally falling into a deep, but troubled sleep. Then she had slept much later than she had wanted.

The weight of her situation with Evan and Artemis lay heavy upon her chest with an almost physical pain. She had to make amends with Artemis. And she had to get through to Evan somehow, to make him see that they belonged together. His words had wounded her deeply. Surely she did not bring out the worst in him. He was not the same hotheaded young man he had been when they first met and fell in love.

She had always considered his jealousy and over-protectiveness endearing and romantic. Even though he ran with a Corinthian set, he exhibited what was commonly considered poetic behavior. She had been young then, too young to understand that Evan had a genuine problem with his jealous temper. After seven years, she never thought about his faults. She remembered only the good in him. It never dawned on her that he might have tried to reform his ways. She had not known until seeing him again that it had caused him such distress.

It gave her some hope that his feelings for her were strong, but being blamed as the cause of his rampages of envy made her despair. Evan had matured to become a gentleman worthy of his title. She had to prove to him that he could love her and not revert to the man he had once been. But how?

She rose from her bed as her maid entered the room with a tray. "Bonjour, Madame."

"Babette, I shall forego my chocolate for now. I believe I might be running late. I do not wish to miss seeing the men heading out for the Quorn."

"Oui, Madame. Zee other maids say zey depart in less than an hour," Babette informed her.

"Then I am indeed late. Why did you not wake me?"

"You were sleeping so sound, I did not 'ave the heart to wake you."

"Thank you, Babette." Miranda said. The girl she had brought with her from London was a good lady's maid, but she tended to follow some of her own ideas. "Now help me get dressed."

"Oui, bon."

In a mere thirty minutes, Miranda exited her bed-chamber with both nervousness and excitement pumping in her veins. She had never seen a hunting party ride out, and she very much looked forward to the Rothwell tradition of the ladies waving the men on their way.

The tradition held that the ladies walked the entire drive waving their handkerchiefs. The riders might then stop and take a lady's bit of linen as a token of good fortune. Miranda did not want to miss the chance to wish Evan well. And she needed to speak to Artemis if she could.

Miranda descended the main stairs quickly. She joined the ladies gathered in the entrance hall, their linen handkerchiefs in hand.

"Good, Miranda, you are here," Beatrice said. "Let us go, then. The gentlemen have already mounted their horses."

"But where is Artemis?" Miss Whitlow asked.

"She said she had the headache and is staying abed," Beatrice explained, as she caught Miranda's eye.

Miranda felt almost relieved at the news. She could at least see Evan off without worrying about keeping her distance in front of Artemis. If Evan ignored her offering of a handkerchief, she would know that he planned to make amends with Artemis and proceed with the betrothal.

Miranda followed the women down the long drive as the gentlemen mounted their proud hunters. The horses pranced and pawed at the ground, eager to be gone, but the choosing of a lady's handkerchief was at hand.

Miranda's stomach flipped over as she spotted Evan sitting tall and serious upon his hunter. Her nerves felt tight as a bowstring stretched to the breaking point. She could not break down in the Rothwells' drive if Evan chose to ride past her.

She could not let the turmoil inside her show. Evan needed his mind sharp as he galloped over hill and hedge. Foxhunting was often dangerous, and Miranda did not want Evan's thoughts distracted by a display of poor emotions on her part. She wanted him to return whole and unbroken.

The morning was clear with a stiff breeze—a perfect autumn day. The men waited as the ladies spread out along the length of the drive, waving their handkerchiefs. Miranda was suddenly caught up in the moment, and she cheered and waved with all her might. She must appear strong, regardless of what happened.

The men started their processional, each one holding back his mount from bolting. The horses appeared to know this tradition as well. They stamped their feet and snorted with impatience to be on their way. The deep sound of baying hounds could be heard in the far distance. The huntsman was no doubt herding his hounds in preparation. Soon, when all the riders had arrived in the village of Quorn, he would let them loose, and the hunt would commence.

Rothwell stopped in front of Beatrice, who reached up on her tiptoes for a kiss from her husband. He raised her handkerchief to his nose to inhale its scent before tucking it into his waistcoat pocket. Other gentlemen stopped in front of other ladies, and Miranda watched with delight. She envisioned Rothwell Park as it might have been in medieval times before a tournament. She could easily cast the men in riding clothes as knights wearing armor and parading their family crests upon their shields.

Mr. Clasby slowed his horse in front of Miranda, much to her dread. The last thing she needed to do was revive Evan's jealousy. She let out the breath she had been holding when she saw Evan nod to Clasby to move along.

She wondered if he had looked for Artemis. Perhaps Beatrice had told him that she was abed ill.

Finally, Evan stopped in front of Miranda. His hunter threw his head in protest of the delay, and Miranda kept her distance.

"It is quite safe," Evan said. "He will not harm you."

Miranda cautiously stepped up to the horse to stand near Evan's boot. She shielded her eyes from the brightness of the sun that had come from behind a puffy white cloud. She looked up at him. "Please be careful," she said in earnest.

"I promise I will." He looked concerned and added cautiously, "Are you well this morning?"

Miranda felt her throat grow tight. She would not cry! She nodded and smiled. He seemed satisfied with that, and so she handed him her handkerchief. It was a silken, lace-edged thing that was completely useless for any practical task. "Very well, then," she said, "take this for luck."

He tucked the filmy cloth into his waistcoat pocket and gave her a wink before he trotted down the drive with the rest of the men, leaving her to hope that all would indeed turn out as she hoped.

She stood gazing after him for some time before she realized that Beatrice was speaking to her, and they were completely alone in the drive.

"He's a good rider, Miranda. He'll be fine." Beatrice put an arm around her.

"Bea, did you talk to Artemis?"

Beatrice gave her a squeeze. "We spoke a little last night."

Miranda pulled out of the embrace and faced Beatrice. "What did she say?"

"We talked of many things, and truly, Miranda, I do not believe her feelings are deeply engaged. She is being stubborn right now, declaring that she will not release Ashbourne from his offer. But I believe she accepted Ashbourne because her father approves of him. Rothwell is rather insanely happy about the match, and he rushed it along once Artemis gave him her agreement. Still, I do not think she will truly go through with this and wed.''

Miranda breathed a shade more easily. ''And now she has the headache,'' Miranda pointed out. ''Do you think she will ever forgive me?''

''Of course she will, with time. She is angry, and hurt, but I think she will heal. Now more than ever, I want her to have a Season in London this spring. If for no other reason, I want to expose her to the outside world. She needs to spread her wings and realize her worth is far greater than her ability with horses and a bow and arrow. Before, that was enough for her; now such talents fall short of bolstering her confidence in herself as a young lady.''

Miranda nodded in agreement. Poor Artemis. It was not easy to face one's shortcomings. ''Perhaps I should look in on her and see how she fares. I do hope that she will talk to me.''

Beatrice smiled. ''Yes, but be prepared if she refuses to see you. She feels a bit sensitive just now.''

Miranda nodded. ''Has Evan spoken to Rothwell?'' she asked.

''No. Rothwell slept so soundly I did not have the heart to wake him. They will no doubt share a coze this evening.''

Miranda nodded, feeling completely unworthy of Beatrice's kindness. For the last two days, Miranda had viewed Artemis as a rival, rather than the tenderly awkward young woman she was. She had to make it up to her somehow.

She walked arm in arm with Beatrice into the main

house, feeling more hopeful than she had felt last night. Miranda was indeed lucky to have such an understanding friend. She only hoped Rothwell would take the news as well.

Miranda went up the stairs in search of Artemis and knocked lightly upon the girl's door. Hearing no answer, she peeked her head inside, calling softly.

No response.

She stepped into the room and looked about. The bed was unmade, and the room looked as if Artemis had left in a hurry.

A feeling of uneasiness stole over Miranda. She had a terribly bad feeling about Artemis' absence. She tried to shake her trepidation away, considering that perhaps the girl had gone in search of peace and quiet. Miranda knew the place where Artemis would retreat. She hoped and prayed the girl would indeed be there.

Miranda headed back down the stairs and out of doors across the drive and yard into the deserted stables. The only sound she heard was that of the few horses left behind munching hay. She walked the aisles quickly, looking in each stall, when a bundle of cloth in the corner of an empty stall caught her eye. Miranda read the brass nameplate affixed to the door, and with fear, she realized where Artemis had gone.

Stepping into the stall belonging to Artemis' mare, Miranda picked up the bundle of clothes and shook them out. It was one of Artemis' riding habits. "Oh dear," she said aloud. Artemis had gone to join the hunt, and Miranda would lay odds that the clothes the girl wore were decidedly masculine.

Miranda stood frozen with indecision as she considered her options. She could alert Beatrice and throw the entire household into an uproar that would only give more fodder to the spiteful Waterton-Smythe sisters. Artemis needed no more damaging tales spread about.

Or, she could go after Artemis on her own. If anyone found out that Artemis had joined the Quorn, her reputation would certainly suffer, but if, as Miranda suspected, Artemis had gone dressed as a man, her reputation would be in shreds. Secrecy was essential. Miranda had promised to make it up to Artemis. Now was her chance. She was not about to let her or Beatrice down again.

Beatrice! Miranda nearly panicked, until she thought of the perfect little fib.

She rushed out of the stables and headed straight for her room, where she quickly changed into her riding habit. Somehow she would find Artemis and bring her back home before she was discovered. Her disguise would buy her only so much time, since eventually someone was bound to figure out that Artemis was no boy.

Once changed and ready, Miranda scribbled a brief note to Beatrice explaining that she and Artemis had gone for a ride. She added a further scribble not to expect them back before luncheon and handed it to a servant on her way out. Crossing the yard to the stables once again, Miranda gestured to the stable boy cleaning stalls.

"Young man," she said. "I need your help in saddling one of Lord Rothwell's mounts as quickly as possible."

"But ma'am, Lord Rothwell's horses are all out to pasture."

She stood perplexed. It would take too much time to fetch the creatures. She looked about until her gaze rested upon one of Evan's horses. "I will take Lord Ashbourne's then."

The boy looked skeptical, almost fearful of obeying her. "Even the grooms dinna want to ride that one, ma'am."

"Quickly! I have not the time to waste," Miranda snapped. "I shall take full responsibility."

The boy pulled his forelock and quickened his step to do her bidding.

Finally, Miranda was in the saddle, but since the horse had refused a sidesaddle, she was forced to ride astride. It was awkward and a bit uncomfortable at first, but she soon grew accustomed to it. The skirts of her habit were full enough to keep her legs respectably covered. But if she were discovered, her actions would draw considerable comment, regardless of her modest appearance.

She urged Evan's mount forward, but she dared not gallop down the main drive. She must appear calm to anyone who might be looking. Veering to the right, she took a trail that ran well behind the main house, one she had taken early in her visit. The trail met with the main road leading to Quorn.

Evan circled his hunter for the second time as he waited for the Master of the Quorn, George Osbaldeston, to finish his lengthy speech. Several of the horses bucked and reared in anticipation of the run ahead.

"For pity's sake, get on with it, man," an onlooker called out from the crowd.

Osbaldeston blustered, as those gathered cheered in agreement. Finally, Osbaldeston gave the signal to the huntsman to let loose his pack. The field followed, as the huntsman's pack of hounds sniffed their way to a covert. The change in pitch from baying to shrill barks announced the fox's presence. The hounds raced along the brushy sedge until they drew the fox out.

"Tally ho!" the huntsman shouted.

Evan tensed his muscles in excitement, ready to spur his mount into a mad gallop. There was nothing like a good hunt on a clear day with the smell of fallen leaves in the air.

The fox shot out of the long thicket followed by the hounds, and the hunt was on. Evan squeezed the sides of his hunter, and the two moved as one with one goal: follow the dogs.

The mass of riders sped across the field, through a thicket of woods, over a stream, and down a hill into open farmland. On and on they rode with bruising speed. One man was tossed from his saddle to land in an injured heap upon the ground when they cleared a hedgerow; another's horse twisted its leg in a hole and would no doubt have to be shot.

Foxhunting was not for the faint at heart. As he and the rest of the hunt followed the hounds streaming across the field, he felt the excitement pumping through his veins. He slowed his horse to a canter as he entered the Charnwood Forest. Through a copse of trees he noticed a rider atop a much smaller horse thundering past him.

Blast, but he knew that horse! It was Artemis' mare. Who the devil had taken her out? He'd wager the head groom would have the undergroom's hide.

Evan urged his mount forward in order to come up next to the rider. Surely it was not one of the guests? And then he saw the long tendrils of dark brown hair escaping from under her hat.

It was Artemis.

His blood boiled. "What the deuce do you think you are doing?" he yelled.

She gave him a startled look, but then, with a cheeky grin, she spurred her mare on to dart dangerously fast through the trees.

Evan shook his head. She'd break her neck if he did not do it for her when he caught her.

After clearing the densest part of the forest, the fox turned north toward Shepeshed, and the pack followed. They would soon cross over Rothwell's land. Artemis could easily fall behind and go home without being discovered. He urged Elias into a gallop and followed Artemis' mare. The deuce, but that mare was fast!

He chased her a good three miles before he could gain enough speed upon open land to bring his hunter up next to her. He reached out and roughly pulled on her reins, bringing the mare to a jerky halt. His horse did not appreciate his actions and reared up. Evan struggled to balance himself in order to stay in the saddle without letting go of Artemis' reins. The mare's eyes nearly rolled back with fright.

When Evan managed to bring his own horse under control, he turned to Artemis with barely concealed fury. "Are you trying to get yourself killed?"

"I was just fine until you came along," she snapped back at him.

"You were not fine. Your mare is frothing at the bit, and you are close to ruining your reputation."

"Why should I care?"

"First and foremost, anyone with a shred of decency would care for her horse. Second, if you had any thought for your parents' well-being, you'd not risk the good name of Rothwell on such a stunt as this." Evan saw that his scold had hit home. The

defiance went out of her like a change in the wind.
"Come on, let's get out of the path of the other
riders."

He never let go of the mare's reins, since he did
not trust her. She might dart off again. The thundering sounds of hoof beats echoed across the open field
as the rest of the riders came barreling through the
grass. He looked at Artemis woeful expression, and
his anger softened. "You rode very well, Artemis.
You have nothing to prove, you know."

Her lower lip began to tremble. "It is not that."

"Then what is it? You could have broken your
neck out there. One gentleman has been seriously
hurt this morning when he fell from his horse. What
makes you think it could not happen to you? Your
parents would be inconsolable if you were hurt."

Guilt was beginning to show in her eyes. "I
know."

"Then, why? If anyone were to see you dressed as
a man, you'd be hard pressed to hold your head up
high again. It would be talked of for years. Men like
Ranton would never allow you or others to forget
your lapse in respectability."

Artemis' head hung even lower. "After last night,
I wanted to impress you. I wanted to show you that
I could hunt the Quorn as well as any man."

Evan lifted her chin with his finger. "Artemis, I
have already said that you ride better than many
men I know. You needn't prove that to me."

"But I cannot compete as a lady. I am not accomplished or beautiful like Miranda. She is the one you
kissed, not I. Only in this"—she gestured broadly
across the field—"do I excel."

Evan closed his eyes. The blame could be laid at
his own feet. He had sent her a note of apology ask-

ing that she make time for them to discuss the matter later today. He had dealt with both Artemis and Miranda unfairly. He feared Miranda was right: Artemis deserved better than he could give her. He did not love her and doubted he ever would. But he was in no position to cry off, as that would also ruin Artemis' good name. It was a fine kettle of fish he'd got himself into.

"Come, let us go home," he said finally, with a sigh.

"But you cannot bow out of the hunt now," Artemis argued.

"I find that I do not have a taste for it." Evan turned his horse in time to see a lone rider literally flying across the fields. It was a woman, and she rode his horse, the young one. The horse was too green and skittish for even experienced groomsmen to ride.

"Who is that?" Artemis whispered.

The woman pulled back on the reins as the horse approached a hedgerow at breakneck speed. She was not going to make that jump! With a sinking feeling, Evan knew the rider's identity.

Miranda!

His heart seemed to halt as he watched, frozen in fear. It happened in an instant. Pulled back hard, his young hunter reared up on his hind legs. He heard Artemis' gasp as Miranda fell hard to the ground and then lay there in terrible stillness.

He moved as if part of him was left behind still watching. He kicked his hunter into action, and they sped across the distance to where Miranda lay. His young horse, realizing it had lost its rider, stood nearby, pawing fretfully at the ground.

Evan was out of his saddle in a trice. He prayed that she was unharmed, but his worst fears were realized when he spied Miranda twisted in a heap at the base of the hedgerow. Her eyes were closed and her skin looked pale. Time stopped, and a haze blurred his vision. *"No!"* He had screamed it aloud.

He knelt down and felt for her pulse. He felt the life beating steadily under his fingers, and he almost fainted with relief. She was alive!

"Oh, no—oh, no." Artemis stood behind him, whimpering.

"Go for help, Artemis. Ride home, and get a gig. Tell your mother to send for a surgeon." When she wavered, Evan yelled, "Go! Now!"

She did as bid, and Evan turned his attention back to Miranda. He chafed her hands, smoothed her forehead, and called her name, but still she did not wake. He looked around them to ensure they were out of danger from the hunt. He detected the sound of baying hounds in the far distance. They'd not be back through here any time soon.

He stripped off his coat and covered her with it. His waistcoat came next, which he placed beneath her head. Then he held her hand and waited for help to arrive.

He sat there watching the shades of light through the hedgerow move across her pale skin, and he began to shake. He could not prevent the feeling of complete helplessness from overtaking him, threatening to choke him. If she died, the fault would be his.

He had set these wheels in motion when he first kissed Miranda. He had let things spiral out of control to arrive at this pass. He brought her limp hand to his cheek, feeling tears burn his eyelids. She was beautiful even as she lay there unconscious.

"God, please make her well," he choked.

Chapter Thirteen

Miranda woke with a throbbing head and aching muscles. She lay still, her limbs feeling as if they were made of lead. She opened one eye, testing how her head would react to the entrance of light. But the room was dark, save for the soft glow of a candle burned down nearly to its base.

She opened the other eye and looked around, realizing she was in her bedchamber at Rothwell Park. Evan sat in a rocking chair, a book open in his lap and his head against the high back of the chair. His eyes were closed. He still wore his riding clothes and clenched in his hand was the silk handkerchief she had given him just this morning.

She smiled as she noticed that his short hair stuck out in places, and that small movement hurt. "Oh," she groaned.

Evan's eyes flew open. In moments he knelt at her bedside. "Miranda, thank God," he whispered as he took up her hand and brought it to his lips.

"How did I get here?" Her voice was hoarse. "What happened?"

"You suffered a terrible fall. You could have been killed." His voice rose slightly. "What on earth were you thinking?"

She ignored him. "What of Artemis? Is she safe?"

"Yes," he answered. He still held her hand, and his thumb made delicate circles on her palm.

She found the contact disturbing, distracting her thoughts from the questions she needed to ask, the things she needed to know. "Did anyone find out about her riding in the Quorn?"

"No," Evan said. "When she returned home for help, she threw her riding habit over the breeches she wore. Evidently you had given Lady Rothwell a note that the two of you had taken a ride. That was quite astute of you. No one knows that either of you were riding with the Quorn, since Artemis was quick enough to say only that you had fallen from your horse." He stood and slowly paced the floor. "Miranda, what possessed you to take my young hunter? That horse hasn't been put through his paces. You could have been killed."

"So you have already said," Miranda answered. "I did not want Artemis' reputation harmed. I felt responsible for her flight, since it was I that you kissed in the stables. I had to find her and try to protect her from ruin."

"You could have been riding for hours and never found her." He stood near her bed, looking down upon her with an oddly anxious expression. "The deuce! If we had not found you when you fell . . ." He did not finish and looked away, raking his fingers through his hair.

"I am quite safe now, Evan. I am fine, can't you see?" She tried to rise up on her elbows, only to see stars dancing about her line of vision. She sank back into her pillows, dizzy and swamped with nausea.

"For the love of Heaven, do not attempt to get up. You will cast up your accounts."

She kept her eyes closed in an attempt to keep the bile at bay. He was right; she would never make it to a sitting position tonight. "How long must I lie here?"

"The surgeon said that, by some miracle, nothing was broken. You are terribly bruised, however. You knocked yourself senseless when you hit the ground."

"Thank goodness for the hardness of my head, once again." She opened her eyes in time to see his rueful smile.

"You have a concussion," he said in all seriousness. "You must lie still and rest for at least a couple of days."

"What time is it?" It was completely dark outside her window.

"Nearing nine o'clock. You have been out since the accident."

"And you stayed with me?"

She saw the color rise to his cheeks. "Yes. Lady Rothwell has been in and out, and Artemis, too."

"Where is she?"

"I did what I knew you would wish. I shooed her off to the Quorn Ball. Clasby will look after her."

Miranda settled into her pillow, feeling drowsy. "Thank you," she whispered. "And thank you for staying with me." Her eyelids became exceedingly heavy, and she drifted back to sleep, certain now that everything would work out between them.

Evan watched her sleep, thankful that the color had returned to her face. She looked peaceful. The bruised bump on her forehead, however, was not a pretty sight. She'd not like it when she saw it. He brushed back her hair with a tentative hand. She had escaped a dreadful fall relatively unharmed. It could have been worse, much worse.

The thought that she might have died did not sit

well with him. In fact, it caused him such distress that he felt stripped of any sense of control upon his feelings. In fact, he didn't know if he'd rein them into submission ever again. He was afraid to leave her side in case she was injured more seriously. The whole time she slept he had checked constantly to make sure that she breathed. He could not have rested until she became conscious.

He walked to her window and looked out into the moonless night. The blackness was pierced only by the lantern lights shimmering along the drive. He had been wrong. He still would not rest easy. He had this mad urge to steal Miranda away and keep her locked up where she could never harm herself again. He knew she would never stand for such over-protective behavior. Had she not told him that Crandle had more or less done just that?

He rubbed his temples. Why was he cursed with this obsession for her? He could not hope for a cure if he let himself love the very person who caused such moments of insanity. It would simply start all over again, would it not?

"Ashbourne?" Lady Rothwell placed a hand upon his shoulder.

He nearly jumped. He had not heard her enter.

"Please, Cook has dinner for you. I will sit with Miranda."

"She woke up for a short time."

Lady Rothwell's face broke into a smile of relief. "Oh, thank goodness. That is a very good sign. All the more reason for you to go and eat, and change into more comfortable clothes."

He looked down. His riding clothes were dirty. He must look a mess. "I suppose you are right. I am in sore need of a bath."

"Go, then. I will have supper sent to your room."

"Thank you, ma'am."

"Please, you must call me Beatrice." She gestured with her hands for him to take his leave. "I will send for you if she wakes again. Is that fair?"

"Indeed it is, Beatrice, as long as you agree that I will be the one to sit with her through the night."

"Of course, I would not expect otherwise." Again she smiled, and then, as if contemplating her next words, she said softly, "Perhaps Miranda is the answer to what you seek."

Evan cocked his head as if trying to understand what she meant.

"Go, now, but give my words thought."

"Dear lady, I promise that I will." Evan left the room, looking forward to a hot soak in a tub and a warm meal. Beyond that, he had not the strength to examine.

Miranda slept through the next day. She woke a couple of times, only to fall back to sleep once she realized that Evan was nearby. He gave her a sense of security that allowed her not to think of anything other than getting well. It was Wednesday before she finally sat up without succumbing to dizziness, and she felt as weak as a two-day old kitten.

Evan had remained by her bedside for two full nights. When she woke this morning, she firmly chased him out, lest he make himself ill. He had darkened smudges of tiredness and worry under his eyes.

She wiggled her toes under the coverlet in anticipation of breakfast. Her room remained dark in the dull gray light; the day was overcast and threatening rain. The gentlemen continued to hunt, except for Evan.

He had insisted that Rothwell ride Elias. It was well known that Evan had purchased two of his three horses used to foxhunt from Rothwell; perhaps Rothwell's hunters might still sell.

Evan had revealed to her that George Osbaldeston was nearly beside himself with fury when Rothwell showed up riding a horse originally bought from the Rothwell stables instead of being forced to hire one of Osbaldeston's prime pieces of horseflesh.

Miranda was pleased to see that Evan had let the matter drop entirely. It served no purpose to risk a duel when there was no proof of sabotage. Evan did not force the issue with Rothwell either, since his hunters were recovering nicely and enjoying their time at pasture. Whether the fellow named Gerald had something to do with it or not, she was not about to bring the whole thing up again.

She snuggled further down into the bevy of pillows that cushioned her as she sat up in bed. Her head still ached, but not as severely. The main hurt was the lump on her forehead. It was an enormously ugly thing, but she could not be cross since, as Evan had said repeatedly, she could have been killed.

"Good morning." Artemis came through the opened door, following the maid who brought her tray.

"Good morning to you," she said, feeling disappointed when she noticed that her morning meal was nothing more than thin porridge, a slice of toasted bread, and tea. "Are there no eggs?"

Artemis laughed, then sat down in the rocking chair. "Mama hoped you would be hungry but insisted that anything heavy might make you sick."

The maid positioned the tray next to the bed and poured the tea.

Miranda swirled her spoon in the porridge, releasing tendrils of sweet smelling steam. She took a bite. "Mmmmm," she murmured. It was surprisingly good. "Is there honey in this?" she asked.

"Probably. Cook keeps bees, and she tries to put honey in everything."

After the maid had left, Artemis came to sit upon the side of her bed. Nervously, she fidgeted with the bed cover. "Miranda, I do not know how I can possibly beg your forgiveness."

Miranda took a sip of her tea. "Artemis, I understand that as an experienced rider, you must have found it exciting to ride in the Quorn."

"That is not why I did it." Artemis would not meet her gaze.

"Then, why, dearest? Why risk your reputation in such a way?"

"I no longer cared for my reputation. I wanted to win at something," she hesitated, then quietly added. "I wanted to win Ashbourne from you."

Miranda reached out to touch her hand. "Oh, Artemis."

"You are so beautiful and accomplished, and I"— Artemis shook her head—"I was wrong, and I hope you will forgive me."

Miranda's heart was indeed touched, but it also beat hard with hope. "Of course you are forgiven, but I am the one who must ask for *your* forgiveness."

"I shall not go through with my betrothal to Lord Ashbourne," Artemis said.

Miranda let out a sigh of relief. "Are you quite sure?" She could not believe she was asking Artemis to rethink her position.

"Yes, I am certain."

"Other than the dreadfully awkward moment in the stables, what changed your mind?"

"I do not quite know. I fully intended to have him, even after coming upon you both in the stable. But when I saw you lying so still, everything became crystal clear. I do not love Ashbourne. I have been acting like a spoiled child. I do not even know who I am, really. And so I should very much like to find out. If your offer to sponsor me in London during the Season still stands, I would like to take you at your word and go."

Miranda did not know what to say, so she said nothing. She merely opened her arms wide to embrace Artemis, who returned the gesture. They clung to each other for longer than necessary as they each forgave the other.

"I will not stand in your way, Miranda," Artemis said, when she pulled back. "You may have Lord Ashbourne with my blessing."

Miranda played with the ends of the girl's hair. "You cannot imagine how much it means to me to hear you say that. And I humbly beg your pardon for kissing your betrothed."

Artemis giggled. "Of course I forgive you. He was quite worried, you know. He sat at your bedside every night. He truly cares deeply for you. It is with you that he belongs."

Miranda felt almost giddy with joy. If her accident became a blessing in disguise, then she was indeed grateful. She absently felt the knot on her forehead. It was painfully sore to the touch but worth every ache if it had brought Evan to his senses. Would he come to her with a declaration of love, or would she have to convince him to act on his feelings?

"Have you spoken to your father, then?" Miranda asked.

"Yes." Artemis hung her head.

"What happened?" Miranda nibbled on her toast.

"He was not in the least happy. Thank goodness he had not sent the announcement to the *Morning Post*."

"There will be some repairing to do," she cautioned.

"I know." Artemis swung her hair, which she had left unfettered to fall freely past her shoulders. "But Mama says that it will not be too difficult to overcome jilting a man like Ashbourne."

Miranda nodded slowly. *Oh dear, she had not considered that.* Several of the guests would no doubt take this juicy bit of gossip back to London. But at least Artemis was young and untried, considering she had not yet experienced a Season. She should not suffer too bad a dent in her reputation. All would be forgotten in time.

The two of them spent the rest of the morning chatting about plans for Artemis' upcoming Season, until Miranda grew tired. Artemis left so that Miranda could take a much needed nap. Miranda was very pleased with the way things had turned out, and she felt blessed to have such dear friends. She believed Artemis was sincere in her desire to go to London. Miranda looked forward to it as much if not more than her young charge. Miranda was not about to let the Rothwells down this time. She would indeed plan a very proper come-out for their daughter.

Later that day, a knock at the door drew Miranda's attention away from the book she read. "Come in," she called, eager for another visitor. Miss Whitlow had been the only lady other than the Rothwells who had called upon her.

"How are you feeling?" Evan entered her chamber with a tray laden for tea.

"Much better, I thank you." She looked for Babette to follow, but Evan was alone.

"I hope you do not mind that I sent your servant on her way. I wished to speak with you, if you are feeling up to it."

Nervous excitement flooded through her. *He was finally going to express his true feelings for her!* She smoothed the coverlet over and over. "Of course."

"I think that bump will look worse before it gets better," he said.

Her hand subconsciously reached for her forehead. She had tried to arrange her hair to cover it, but it proved difficult since the bruise was spreading as it healed. The skin surrounding the lump had turned an ugly purplish green. "It is an eyesore, is it not?" She tried to be humorous, but her voice faltered.

"It is not so bad. I am grateful that you fared no worse."

"As am I." She felt overwhelmingly shy in his presence, which was remarkable. She had never felt thus before. She cleared her throat. "What did you wish to discuss?"

Evan awkwardly poured the tea for them both, before answering her. "I need your advice." He handed her a cup of tea, then sat down in the chair next to her bed.

"On what, pray tell?" She took a sip.

He looked away. "Artemis," he said.

Miranda's heart sank. "What of her?"

Evan sat forward and set his cup down. "You were

correct. We do not suit, and I find myself at a loss as to how to withdraw. It will ruin her."

Miranda leaned back, cup in hand, her spirits restored. "Do not worry. Speak to Rothwell."

"I am unsure how best to approach him."

"Evan, you need not worry. Artemis will not accept you. She has already informed her father."

Evan nodded. "I am glad." He picked up his cup of tea and sipped it. Instead of looking relieved, he remained quiet and tense.

There was more to be discussed. She drew in a deep breath. The time to broach the subject of her feelings for him had finally come. She wanted to tell him that she loved him, but she was suddenly afraid. He had not yet declared himself.

"You were right all along." His voice was soft, apologetic, as it cut the heavy silence.

"About Artemis?" she asked.

"About a lot of things." He looked her straight in the eye. "But I need peace and calm, Miranda."

Dread spilled into her, causing her to tremble. She did not like the look in his eye. "Yes, many seek peace, but I do not know what you mean by calm."

He set down his tea with a clink on the small table near her bed and rose to his feet. He raked a hand through his hair, tousling it into disarray. He could not have looked more attractive or vulnerable. He walked to the window. "You nearly granted me an intimate relationship the other night."

"But I did not. I wanted to, but not with your intentions toward Artemis hanging between us," she said boldly. "Now that that has been put to rights."

"Do not say it," he interrupted her.

"Why? Why can I not say what I have longed to say for seven years. Evan, I love you," she said.

His shoulders slumped, and he leaned his head against the glass of the window.

"Is that so bad?" she asked frantically. Why did he act distressed by her declaration?

He turned and faced her. "For me it is."

"How can that be?"

He walked back to the chair and pulled it closer to her bedside. Taking both her hands into his own, he sat down with a sigh. "Do you not remember when we first met how furiously jealous I was?"

"Yes, you called out my cousin."

"Because I saw him kiss you."

"It was merely a friendly family buss on the cheek," Miranda defended.

"Exactly! Completely harmless, and yet I raged like a madman."

"Evan," Miranda soothed. "You were young and foolish."

"But I still rage." He pointed to his chest. "In here, the madness is still inside. I cannot bear to see another man touch you. I nearly came unhinged when I heard you and Clasby laughing outside the church."

Miranda squeezed his hands. "But you did not challenge your friend. You did not react as you would have years ago."

"I was cruel to you."

"Yes, but even so. Evan, you are aware of your weakness, and you are trying to correct it. That shows maturity."

"Miranda," he said. "You do not understand. I want to avoid it. If I were to allow myself to become involved with you, I do not know if I could continue to control my temper. I do not wish to live my life under the threat of such insanity." He dropped her hands and stood up again. "When I saw you fall—"

His voice grew thick. "When I saw your ashen face, I thought you were dead, and that feeling—upon my soul, it nearly tore me in two. I have not been the same since."

She stared at him and he at her. She felt extremely tired, as if she had just walked for miles and yet still had not reached her destination. She had no idea how to overcome his objections.

"Evan, earlier this week you told me that you would show me what I had chosen to give up. You tried to punish me for choosing Crandle."

He hung his head. "Forgive me. I had no right."

She held up her hand. "Please, stop. You were correct. I needed to feel what it was like to kiss you again. I needed to feel alive again. Evan, you cannot go through the rest of your life deadening your love because you are afraid of the intensity of your emotions."

"It is more than just emotions. You have always been an obsession for me, one I fear will take over who I have become. I cannot abide feeling so out of control." He retreated back to the safety of the window. "The deuce, when you leave a room, I wonder how long it will be until you return. This whole time I courted poor Artemis, it was you that I looked for each time I entered a room. It was you who caused my hands to ache with wanting to touch you."

Miranda could not believe her ears. He professed his adoration, and yet he feared to love her. She threw the coverlet back and slid out of bed to walk toward him. "Then touch me, Evan, and get it over with. I will not destroy you. I will complete you just as you complete me. I have waited my whole life for you, and then because of Crandle I had to wait yet again. This time, there can be no other, and I refuse to wait."

He shook his head. "Miranda, get back to your bed. You threaten your recovery."

She stamped her foot with impatience. "Evan, you *are* my recovery! These last seven years, part of me died when I left you to marry Crandle. You have brought that part of me back to life—the part that feels young and laughs, the part that gets nervous with gooseflesh at the very thought of a kiss." She stood before him now, her hands resting on his chest. "I will not let that part die again, not without a fight."

"Botheration, but you fight well," he said, just before he brought his lips down upon hers.

Miranda clung to him as he wrapped his arms about her and pulled her close. His lips moved desperately over hers, as if he tried to memorize her mouth. He moaned as if in pain, and Miranda's heart stopped. This kiss was his goodbye. He kissed her as if there would be no more kisses.

She pushed away from him, furious. "You did not hear a word I said."

His eyes glittered with emotion—need, sorrow, and regret were wrapped into one doleful expression. "Miranda, I need some distance, some time."

"You have had seven years distance from me; why do you hesitate now?" She shook her head. "In fact, why did you even remain unwed these seven years? Was it because of me?"

His brow furrowed heavily. "No. I had my estate to put in order first. That is what I am trying to explain to you. I have lived an orderly life where I alone controlled my destiny. I am not willing to give that up!"

Miranda felt rebuked. The truth had finally come out. He did not fear love; he simply did not wish to give up his own will to make room for another's. "Then you do not love me, Evan. You love only yourself. Please, I am tired, and I wish you to leave."

Evan saw the light go out in Miranda's eyes. He had won. He had finally made her understand why he could not make a future with her. He found no comfort in his victory. In fact, he felt empty inside. He reached out to help her back to her bed, but she shrugged off his touch. She walked regally across the room, her deportment completely at odds with the billowing white nightgown she wore and her bare feet.

She climbed back into bed and lay back with her eyes closed. She did not utter another word. Evan left quietly. He shut her door with utmost care and leaned his forehead against it. He had lost something precious. He wondered if he was right to refuse her this way. Was he making yet another mistake?

Clasby walked by and slapped him on the back. "How is she?"

"She is sleeping now, tired still." His voice was thick.

"You don't look good. Are you all right?"

"The deuce if I know," Evan said with disgust. He walked away, leaving a worried Clasby standing alone outside Miranda's door.

Chapter Fourteen

*T*he next morning, Miranda rose early from her bed with a heavy heart. She needed to leave. She could not bear to be under the same roof with Evan if he refused to see what was right under his nose. If not for his stubborn fear of losing control of his life, they might have a wonderful future.

It hurt and angered her that he had rejected her so. He did not want love, nor did he want a wife. He thought he wanted an heir to carry on his title. Obviously, he had not considered how a family was bound to upset his rigidly controlled existence!

"He is a fool," she fumed quietly.

A knock at the door caused an absurd rush of hope to swell in her chest. It might be Evan, come to tell her that he had reconsidered. "Come in," she called out.

She did not hide her disappointment when Beatrice walked into her room. "What is this about you leaving? Babette told my maid, who came straight to me. Miranda, you cannot be fit to travel."

"I believe that I am. I have languished in bed as the surgeon ordered. Babette accompanies me. If I should fall ill, I shall not be alone."

"Evan has ordered his things readied to leave as

well," Beatrice said quietly. "I take it that the two of you have had words."

"What Evan does from now on holds not the least interest for me," Miranda said, as she rummaged through her personal items.

"I know that is not true. I am surprised that you are running away instead of staying to win him over. Artemis has made it clear to her father that she will not have him. There remains nothing in your path."

Miranda stopped gathering her jewels to face her friend. "What did Rothwell have to say?"

"Nothing, really. He wants Artemis to be happy. I thank you for offering to sponsor her during the Season."

Miranda reached out and gave Beatrice's hand a squeeze. "I am glad to do it, and I think the experience will be good for her. You and Rothwell are welcome to stay with me as well."

"Yes, I know." Beatrice sighed, looking defeated.

"Bea, what is it?"

"Despite the situation with Artemis, I had such hopes for you and Ashbourne."

Miranda turned back to gathering her things. "I did too."

Evan made a final inspection of his trunks as they were loaded into his carriage before it departed. His groom and valet were driving it back to Ash Manor, his estate. Evan needed to ride alone.

"Lord Ashbourne?"

Evan saw Artemis walking swiftly toward him. She wore a smile, and he cringed inside. His conversation with Rothwell had not gone well. He had expected Rothwell to be angry, but he had not been prepared for the stark disappointment.

Rothwell had certainly said everything Evan had expected to be berated for. Evan had been rightly accused of paying court to Artemis while making moon faces at Miranda. Rothwell had raged on about every natural thing a father should when faced with a broken betrothal so soon after the engagement.

But Evan saw through the charade. What bothered Rothwell the most was losing a fellow huntsman from the family. Rothwell had indeed looked forward to much time spent with Evan in the field.

After consideration, Evan supposed he should take Rothwell's reaction as a good sign. It meant that Artemis Rothwell's feelings were not deeply engaged. She would soon get over whatever hurt he had caused her.

He stepped away from the carriage and bowed slightly. "Good morning, Artemis."

"I heard you were leaving, and I wished to speak with you."

"Indeed."

"Might we walk a bit?"

He held out his arm to escort her. "Of course. You lead the way."

They remained silent until they reached the same small garden where Miranda had accosted him several nights ago. He could not believe that so much had happened between them in so short a period of time. It seemed like ages ago that he had arrived, instead of mere days.

"Lord Ashbourne," Artemis said timidly. "I fear I must be frank with you. I know that you spoke to my father about our dissolved engagement."

Evan felt his back stiffen. He had avoided Artemis after Miranda's accident, knowing that they would not suit. He had pretty much avoided everyone. He had sulked through dinner, listening with only half an ear to the glorious stories of the hunt. Most of the guests planned to stay for another day or two of hunting. Even Clasby planned to stay. Evan found that he had lost all interest. "Please, go on," Evan encouraged her.

"I wish you to know that my father will indeed get over all this, as will I. I know you think me a spoiled hoyden. I cannot say that I blame you, especially after my escapade with the hunt." She held up her hand to stop him from interrupting her. "I simply wanted to tell you that I release you with a clear heart. I beg for your continued friendship, however. I want our parting to be of good cheer with no hurt feelings on either side."

Evan smiled, glad he would be able to end his relationship with Artemis on a positive note. "Nicely said. I appreciate your candor, and I thank you for coming to me." He shifted slightly. "I must beg your pardon for not being as straightforward with you."

"But you did not know your own heart. Miranda is the one for you. It is plain as daylight."

He sighed. "It is not quite that simple."

"It need not be complicated either," Artemis said. "Besides, your hazelnut popped instead of burning. You are destined to be together."

"What was that?" He cocked his head to the side.

"One night, several of the girls carved the initials of the gentlemen of our choosing into hazelnuts. We roasted them upon the grate. Those that did not burn in the flames but popped off from the heat and onto the floor promised to be our future husbands. You were the one on Miranda's hazelnuts. In fact, you scored twice."

"I see." Evan scratched his chin. "And Miranda played this game?"

"We all did." Artemis held out her hand. "I thank you, Lord Ashbourne, for saving Miranda's life the other day and for keeping my indiscretion in confidence. I intend to become worthy of your efforts."

Evan took her hand, not in the least surprised at the firmness of her grip. "You, my dear Artemis, will indeed make some man proud to call wife. I wish you the very best, and I promise not to be a stranger to Rothwell Park."

Evan was surprised when she impulsively gave him a hug, before running back to the main house to let her parents know that he was indeed leaving. He would say his goodbyes to Lord and Lady Rothwell, thank them for their hospitality, and then be gone. He'd bear no shame from Artemis' rejection of marriage. Artemis had released him politely, and for that he was grateful.

As he made his way into the house, he could not shake the vision of Miranda sitting upon the floor, surrounded by young misses playing games to predict their future husbands. She had said that he had brought her back to life. As he considered the change from her reserved demeanor when they first arrived to her willingness to play with hazelnuts like a young girl, he realized that she had blossomed back into the woman he had once fallen in love with.

He had not allowed her to make such positive changes in him. In fact, he had never given her a chance.

Miranda's luggage was packed and stacked onto her carriage. She had long since said her goodbyes, and there was nothing left for her to do but climb in and leave. Her hesitation was ridiculous. Her hope that Evan would change his mind and come galloping back into her life was utterly absurd. *He will not come back,* she told herself with a sigh. His decision had been made.

She walked across the stable yard where her carriage stood ready to depart. Babette had fetched a generous basket of refreshments from Cook that took up nearly the whole seat. Beatrice had insisted that Miranda keep her strength up during their trip. There was enough food to eat quite the entire way to the inn where they would stay overnight before going on to London.

She looked about the yard one last time, wishing and hoping beyond sense that Evan would come to her. Babette had told her that he had already left, his carriage having pulled out of the drive two hours ago. Her heart aching, she stepped up onto the first of the carriage steps.

"Miranda, wait."

She felt her heart drop to the pit of her soul at the sound of his voice. With weakened knees, she turned around to see Evan walking out of the stable toward her. "I thought you had left," she said, as calmly as she could manage. Her heart was beating so hard in her chest she thought for certain that Evan could hear it too.

"I have been trying to leave for hours now, but I cannot."

"Why?" Her voice trembled. Hope soared within her.

"Because I keep thinking of you etching my name upon a hazelnut before placing it on the fireplace grate."

Miranda felt her cheeks flush. "Who told you about that?"

"Artemis. So it is true? My hazelnut popped instead of falling into the fire to burn?"

Miranda swallowed. "Yes, it is true. In fact"—she reached into her reticule and pulled out a pillbox encrusted with jewels. She opened the box and pulled out two hazelnuts, each one scorched on the sides—"there were two." She offered them to him.

He took the nuts from her and turned them over to stare at the letter *E* etched into each one. "Do you believe in fate?" His gray eyes searched hers.

"I do now." She stepped forward to stand directly in front of him. "What do you believe?"

He took a deep breath. "I believe that I have been a blind man. You allowed me to touch some part of you, bring it back to life. The Miranda I knew would carve a man's name into a hazelnut, but the Lady Crandle I met when I first arrived would not."

Miranda felt tears gathering behind her eyes. "And?" Her voice choked with joy and hope.

"And I have been thinking, ever since yesterday, that I am trading your generously offered love for a carefully controlled life that is laced with loneliness. The more I thought of returning to it, the more it paled by comparison."

"What are you saying?" she whispered.

Evan got down on one knee, not caring a whit for the dirt that marred his perfect fawn-colored pantaloons. "Miranda, I ask your forgiveness for being a selfish cad. And might I ask your help to make me into a man who will not be ruled by jealousy of his own wife? I cannot promise not to be overly protective. I only ask that you be patient with me. Will you help me to become a better man?"

Miranda's tears fell freely, and she let them fall without shame. "Evan Langley, Earl of Ashbourne, I will gladly become your wife, and indeed I promise to be patient with you," she whispered.

Several of the guests had made their way out of doors and stopped to watch the proposal. She spied Beatrice standing at the head of the drive, wiping her eyes. She heard her maid, still sitting in the carriage, gingerly blow her nose.

Turning her attention back to Evan, she took his hands and pulled him to his feet. "I will do what I can to help you become a better man, as long as you reciprocate and make me a better woman—a woman who is not afraid to enjoy life."

He picked her up and swung her about. "You need very little improvement, my dear," he said, before he kissed her cheek.

Miranda laughed wholeheartedly. "Just you wait and see."

He put her down and kissed her soundly without embarrassment in front of all. "Do you still wish to leave?" he asked, when he pulled back for air.

"No."

"Good. When shall we marry?"

Miranda grinned at him. "Soon. Perhaps we can obtain a special license."

"You said you would be patient with me," he said, with a lopsided grin that made his dimples deepen.

With her fingertip, she traced those devilish dimples, something she had longed to do. "I have waited for an eternity, and now that I have finally caught you, I will not allow you the chance for second thoughts. Perhaps it is *I* who will not let *you* out of my sight."

He laughed, and Miranda thought it the most wonderful sound. "Very well," he finally said. "Let us ask Rothwell what can be done so that we may be wed here," he said.

"Agreed." Miranda took his hand, and they hastened back to the main house amidst cheering guests.

Beatrice greeted them with a warm embrace. "I am so happy. Now, come inside. We must celebrate."

Miranda spent the rest of the day closeted with Beatrice and Artemis, planning her wedding. Her mother and brother had been sent for, as well as Evan's luggage and valet. Evan and Rothwell left to apply for a license from the archbishop.

Rothwell, Miranda later heard from Beatrice, had grumbled about the whole affair, until Beatrice bolstered his spirits with the reminder that Evan would now return often to Rothwell Park, since Miranda would no longer be a stranger to country life. They would have every reason to spend the hunting season in each other's company. The grounds at Ash Manor were well known for prime grouse and pheasant.

That evening, dinner turned into a grand, festive event. The ballroom was opened for dancing, and champagne flowed freely. Artemis positively beamed as she graciously offered a toast to their happiness, much to the approval of the guests and her parents. It seemed that few were bothered by the change of brides.

The only sour expressions to be found in the happy crowd were on the faces of the Waterton-Smythe sisters. They appeared displeased with the fact that Artemis was not being criticized for crying off from her betrothal to an earl. Miranda knew that the interchangeable sisters would not hesistate to cause Artemis trouble wherever they could, come spring in London.

Miranda made a mental note to keep an ear open for the rumors these vicious misses might spread. She would do everything in her power with her vast connections to keep Artemis Rothwell's good name respected.

The following day brought a flurry of activity in preparation for the wedding breakfast that was to be held on the morrow. Miranda was kept busy and away from Evan, who had gone with the men to Quorn for the last day of foxhunting. Her family arrived, and Miranda felt as though she might burst with joy.

Only one thing bothered her conscience, dampening her excitement. She had not told Evan about her plans to sponsor Artemis' Season in London.

Miranda knew that her main residence would change to Ash Manor, but she was not quite ready to give up her London town house. Now that she had Evan, there was no need to hide from who she was or where she had come from. She was simply Miranda again. And soon she would become Lady Ashbourne. Her title of Lady Crandle and her nickname, the "Portrait of Beauty," could fall by the wayside permanently. She would finally marry her only true love, and that gave her considerable peace.

Would Evan agree to accompany her to London? Or worse, would he let her go there without him, if he chose not to go? She stood alone in her chamber, surveying the dress she had chosen to wear as Evan's bride. The dress was made of the finest light green silk. She had had it made on a whim by her seamstress, who said the color would be all the rage. Her dressmaker had a gift for these things.

Miranda had never worn it, since the style was rather young. The blond lace at the sleeves and hem looked too innocent for a widow to wear, but tomorrow it would serve her well. She felt as young and innocent as the gown looked. And she was nervous too.

What would Evan have to say about an entire Season in London? He wanted nothing to do with city life, but then that had been because of her. Should she tell him now and possibly spoil their wedding day with a fight, or should she wait until after they were safely wed to spill the news that she was honor bound to bring out Artemis Rothwell? Miranda absently bit her fingernail and decided to wait until after they had wed.

It was dawn, and Evan was awake. He had spent little to no time with Miranda the day before, and that bothered him. They had rushed into wedding plans, and then he had been whisked away by the men to enjoy his last day as a bachelor upon the field. Afterwards, he had been entombed in the drawing room amidst cheroots and port.

He paced his chamber like a caged animal. He could not seek out Miranda and wake her lest she think something was wrong. And there was nothing wrong, truly, only that he felt nervous as a green schoolboy, confound it!

He stood before the mirror, feeling overwhelmed by a sense of panic. Everything his life had been was about to change, and he hoped he was ready for it. He loved Miranda, by all that was Holy, he did, but he had not even told her! He ran a shaky hand through his hair and looked outside the window.

The morning was a dull gray, and rain threatened.

That was not a good omen, he thought. Rain on one's wedding day did not promise good fortune. Perhaps they moved too quickly. Should they have waited to wed? He backed away from the window to sit upon his bed, his head in his hands. He was simply nervous, and that was all.

He looked up and saw Miranda's hazelnut sitting upon his bedside table. He had taken one, and she had kept the other. He picked up the smooth brown hazelnut with the letter of his first name carved neatly into its shell. Fate had brought them together again. He was not about to shake their destiny with a simple case of prenuptial nerves.

Miranda stood beside her new husband in the quaint old church that was Rothwell Chapel. Evan looked as handsome as she had ever seen him, in dark blue superfine and a starchy white cravat that had been tied to perfection. He appeared nervous at first, but once the ceremony began, he relaxed. In his eyes, she read his love, and she knew this day was the happiest of her life.

The curate blessed their union, along with their newly purchased license. Evan signed his name in the church register, and then he handed her the quill. Their fingers touched, and Miranda shivered. She could not mistake the desire darkening Evan's gaze. She felt the sharp anticipation of their bridal night lace through her insides, and she quickly looked away. She signed her name before she made a cake of herself, ogling her husband.

"You look radiant," Evan whispered, when they had climbed into the carriage. The rain had turned to a fine mist, settling around them like fairy dust.

"I feel radiant." Miranda clasped her husband's

hand and held tight. She wondered if she should broach the subject of the London Season but thought better of it when Evan gently lifted her chin so that he could look deeply into her eyes.

"Miranda," Evan said softly, "I love you, now and for always. Upon my soul, nothing will ever tear us apart again."

She melted into his embrace and returned his ardent kisses, but her conscience pricked her. She had to tell him about her promise to sponsor Artemis in London, and soon.

Evan lifted Miranda into his arms before entering Ash Manor. It was late, but still his servants had lined up to meet them in the drive. They cheered with genuine glee once he stepped over the threshold with his new bride. On a whim, he and Miranda had decided to forego a night at the inn and had traveled on to Ash Manor to spend their wedding night.

Miranda, still nursing the now small lump on her forehead, had slept most of the way in the crook of his arm. He was more than anxious to tuck her beneath the covers of his bed, but first things first. Ash Manor needed to be toured by its new mistress. He set her down upon her feet.

"Madam," he announced, "I welcome you to my humble home—our home now. Do not say a word until you have seen the whole."

He watched her reaction closely as she took in the main entrance. Ash Manor was a bachelor residence, but still he took pride in its upkeep. He knew it could not equal the elegant salons she must be used to in London, but it was spotlessly maintained. Surely she would see that.

As they walked through the halls, inspecting each

room, he nervously awaited her reaction. As instructed, she had given nothing away. She kept her opinion completely to herself until the very last rooms—his private apartments and bedchamber.

"Well, what do you think?" he anxiously asked.

Miranda bit her bottom lip. Evan's home was impressive but terribly dark. Cherry wood and deep brocades and wall coverings filled the place. No lace or flowers or frivolous embellishments could be found. It was in complete contrast to her quite feminine town house in London.

"Evan," she said, "I have to tell you something."

"You don't like it," he said quickly. "Well, perhaps we might change some things."

She reached out to grasp his hand. "No, I love it, truly." She would discuss remodeling ideas later. "We have not yet discussed what we shall do with my town house in Mayfair."

He looked wary, as if concerned that she would bring up such a subject on their wedding night. "We have not, but I am sure it can wait until morning."

She looked about his room. Babette had arranged some of her things on the dressing table. A lacy negligee had been laid out for her on the settee leading to a dressing room. Her gaze stopped at his very masculine bed with its dark blue curtains and coverlet. She was indeed tempted to keep quiet about the upcoming Season, but it was too important. She needed to know his reaction. She needed to find out if he meant what he had said about becoming a better man.

"No, Evan, it cannot wait," she said after taking a deep breath. "I have promised to sponsor Artemis' Season in London. I am honor bound to do so. My hope, my deepest desire is that you will accompany me to London so that we may bring her out together." There, she had said it.

The expression he gave her was one of complete confusion. "And?"

"And that is all. We would have to stay at my town house in Mayfair, which is positively frilly compared to Ash Manor. You will no doubt dislike my taste, but that is another matter. My fear is that you will so completely hate the idea of a Season that you will refuse to go—or refuse to let me go." Now she was rambling.

A slow smile spread across his face, decadently deepening his dimples. "And you worried yourself over this?"

She felt her cheeks grow warm. "Yes, I did. Should I not have?" Her defenses rose slightly. "Considering that you hate London, I was not at all certain what your reaction would be. I did not wish to fight before we were wed, and now, I must know how you feel."

He caressed her cheek. "We really do not know one another well, do we?" he asked softly.

Her knees felt terribly weak as he drew her close. "No, I suppose we do not."

"And now, we have a lifetime to get to know one another quite well," he purred. His hands slowly rubbed her back, until she was pure fire.

"Evan," she tried to sound reasonable. "It is something we must discuss."

"Later, my love. Suffice it to say that I would not dream of letting you go off to London without me." His fingers pulled at the tapes of her gown.

She could not think clearly. "You will go with me, then? My goodness!" she exclaimed, when he kissed a hot trail down her neck.

"Miranda," he said, as he nibbled her now bare

shoulder. "I will go to Hades and back for you. It might just as well be London."

She smiled and let her head fall back in wanton abandon as she ran her fingers through his thick short hair. "Tonight, I need only for you to take me to Heaven."

"Then, by all means, let us go there," he said, as he carried her to the bed.